I0637165

REFLECTIONS OF SILENCE

A CASKET GIRLS VAMPIRE ROMANCE

SILENT SENTINELS DEUT

RAVEN HUSH

Second Edition

Published by Little Quail Press

Edited by Heather Osborne

ISBN Ebook 978-1-922448-74-3

ISBN Paperback 978-1-922448-75-0

Previously published in part as A PORTRAIT IN ASH AND LACE in 2020 by Sofia Aves

ISBN 9798725916164

❀ Formatted with Vellum

HISTORICAL NOTE

HISTORICAL NOTE

During the early 1700s, the King of France sent unwed women to New Orleans, the small township then founded in 1718, as suitable wives for the French male population already residing there. Some of the woman sent across as suitable wives were from families of good standing, while others were selected from orphanages or poor pulled from the streets. Nearly two hundred were convicted criminals relocated from the prison La Force.

These displaced women had many names: the Casquette Girls, Pelican Girls, *fille à la cassette*, or the more familiar Casket Girls for the small, child-coffin sized trunks they carried with all their worldly goods as they crossed oceans to find a new home in what would later become Louisiana.

The Pelican left France in 1704, and heralds one of the girls' commonly used names. There are now festivals held in their honor in the city streets. One such ship arrived in 1728, but many followed over the years. By 1934, a legend of vampirism had wound itself around these wives, who were intended for the trappers and farmers of a fledgling New Orleans. The women were taken to the Ursuline Convent amidst questions of why they carried these tiny caskets and what was stowed inside them.

Naturally, fact turned to rumor and fear inflicted a legend upon the history of orphaned girls torn from their homes. Alighting from the ships, the girls were pale, as most hadn't seen sun for many months. This heightened the existing vampire stories.

The girls were taken to the convent and locked into the third floor on their first night ashore. The windows were boarded shut to prevent the purported vampire girls from inflicting their curse upon the city. Noises and thumps came from the floor above the convent, and the terrified nuns refused to go up and unlock the girls until daybreak. When they did, all they found were empty caskets and boarded windows. The girls were nowhere to be seen.

New Orleans has a history of magic, the culture ripe with a mix of superstitions created by a patchwork of converged cultures. The Casket Girls is one legend amongst many in the city's virile history, and is the inspiration for Gisella and Sebastian's story of shadows, creatures of the night and all the nightmares and forbidden pleasures that might be wielded there...

...and what happens within those darkened spaces.

REFLECTIONS OF SILENCE includes dark and explicit themes and may not be suitable for all readers.

For the monster under every bed...or the one who crawls into yours.

Welcome, or not.

CHAPTER ONE

GISELLA

1735

My first impression of a fledgling New Orleans was uninspiring. Considering my impending marriage, and my new home, I hoped the locale wouldn't be indicative of my new lifestyle. As filthy and crowded as the Parisian docks might have been, they retained an air of elegance, of civilization beneath the thick layer of grime and *la pute* that overpopulated such a place.

Here, mud covered everything. Crud, muck, and sludge, hid beneath another layer of the brown goop. I pressed worn boots into the hard deck of the boat, relishing the relative sturdiness of the surface as passengers left us at other ports, wobbling away on their sea legs. They struggled to keep themselves upright, and that was on solid ground.

While ship life had been my existence these last

months, the thought of being back on land was a welcome one. Though my feet were content with their current placement, my legs quivered, brain and nerves warring in a silent battle.

I hoped whole-heartedly I wouldn't be the exception of my fellow passengers, and find myself on my derriere in the slush.

Sweat tickled my throat, pooling around the neckline of my dress, and ran unceremoniously into the small of my back. The other girls who had traveled with me from Paris—all for the same reason—didn't appear as discomforted.

Or maybe they hid their emotions better. That had never been a strong point for me, much to my father's disdain. Perhaps that was one of the reasons he shipped me halfway around the world in order to be rid of the daughter he no longer wanted.

It wasn't even a good offer. The king's coffers weren't what they had been in the reign of Louis XIV, by any means.

I resisted the urge to swish my tattered parasol through the cloud of insects determined to devour every inch of exposed skin, resolved to present a calm face to the first moments of my new home. The swarm of tiny gnats and jeweled beetles ignored my intentions, nibbling away at the buffet my pale skin afforded them.

I had an inkling I was overdressed but also underprepared for my new life. Though when I only owned a single, well-worn dress, there weren't many options.

Like most of the girls I traveled alongside, I left my homeland wearing my dress, my little casket tucked beneath my arm.

My father had placed me in an abbey, under the care of nuns—no more than a glorified orphanage for the unwanted and unloved—when my mother passed. His madness devolved into a violent thing, and I had been glad to leave the luxurious life I'd been born into.

Then, along with our government and other families in need of funds, my father had sold me as a *suitable wife* to a man I didn't know, in a country where I had no associations or family of any kind.

Bringing culture to the poor shores of the new land.

Or some such rubbish the king's representative uttered when he droned through the official position. I wasn't the only one who nodded off.

My traveling group became known as the Casket Girls. And I was one of them, headed to a home I'd been allocated. To a husband.

I gripped my little box—a morbid, splinter-ridden affair in the shape of a child's coffin—until my fingers found new pinpoints to torture me, and tried to focus on the mess before me...not the one to come when I married a man I didn't know.

The fate of every woman—girl—I traveled alongside.

All but one.

A rumble of chatter rolled over the deck in waves. Sailors, hurtling about in their duties, added a hefty layer of confusion to the commotion. Suddenly, after weeks stuffed into a teapot-sized room, I wanted nothing more than to retreat there, to hide in the dim light, and return to my homeland.

An elbow in my ribs lifted me out of my daze, the cacophony of the ship rushing back to me.

"It's noisy. And not in the least clean." Amy, a girl of English descent with an atrocious accent, hovered at my side, lines creasing her face.

I wanted to tell her not to frown, but with her heritage, wrinkles were a forgone conclusion. "What is it you English say—put on a brave face?"

Amy scowled. "Once we get to the manor house, I won't *have* to be brave. I wouldn't like to have your fate." Her chin tipped up, though her gaze remained a little wild at the edges. "The house will be clean and fresh, with all my things already there. Not like *you*. Don't you wonder who he is?"

"Of course." I stared at the encroaching dock, disregarding the growing nest of worms writhing in my belly. If I ignored the sensation, perhaps I would be able to be as brave as I had suggested to Amy.

Though the trip from France had been somewhat calm—as calm as a three-month voyage could be considered—the quarters were a tight fit. Cabins were shared, though my second companion had rarely spoken throughout our shared journey, hiding from the open air of the deck. Over the weeks, she had faded into a pallid, little person who was soon forgotten by the rest of the ship's occupants.

Though hers was meant to be a single stateroom,

the few passenger beds had been overbooked, and I'd been shunted in with her until space became available amongst the other French girls.

Which happened when one dived overboard, clutching her casket stowed full of rocks, leaving her half of the cabin vacant.

I shared Amy's accommodations for the first part of the trip. An English socialite who missed the parties of her Continental tour, she plied us both with an endless supply of cheap alcohol stashed in her cabin, the cause of many blank nights and headache-ridden mornings.

We talked rubbish of men and gossip, of what to expect when we arrived in New Orleans. In the darkest hours, deep in the stash of contraband she somehow hid from the sailors who offered us a wide berth, she told me stories of her previous husband.

Unlike the rest of the girls we traveled alongside, she wasn't an unmarried virgin. She was, however, an expense to her family, the remnant of a poor match, and thus outcast with the rest of us.

But her stories...I had curled in my thin blanket at nights on board the ship when all others were asleep, listening to her tales, learning more about what happened behind closed doors of a married couple than I could ever want to know.

"He would come to my bedchamber at night—of course we didn't share one. Don't be so naive." Amy tipped her head up in a show of defiance, though her hand gathered her skirts in her fist. "The first night, he was sweet, attentive. Then, he became more demanding, creating slights we both knew I hadn't committed against him for the pure pleasure of throwing me over his knee and spanking my backside in recompense."

"Over your clothes? Did it hurt?" I couldn't help but wonder, trailing my fingers along my thigh over my tangled skirts and bedsheets.

"Of course not, silly." Amy rolled her eyes and giggled, her face stained pink in the flickering light our broken lantern afforded. "He flicked up my skirts, one by one, all business-like, until I lay naked and exposed before him. Then he would squeeze my bottom, tell me how naughty I had been, and then he spanked me. It hurt; oh, how I cried! Sobbing as his hand stung against my poor skin. At the end, he would rub his fingers over my heated rear, tell me how good I had been. Then his fingers would dip lower.

"I liked the pain, you see, and he found out how much I enjoyed his beatings. My new punishment was to perform on his hand until he was satisfied. Sometimes he made me work my body for him all night until I was covered in sweat, shaking and crying..." She shuddered, bunching both hands at the apex of her thighs over her skirts. "Well, the pain was worth what would come after."

Her knowing smile haunted me as I lay awake, guessing what my own future held, unable to question her more. My own embarrassment had heightened as she shifted on her cot on the other side of the cabin's close confines, moaning and rocking with the ship's movement.

Amy knew where she was headed before any of us got on the ship that had taken us from France to the Americas. Her new husband-to-be had already prepared her home, whereas I knew nothing about my arrival. Impossible hopes and dreams plagued my sleepless hours. I quashed them into the tiny box all the girls traveled with, except for Amy, who came accompanied by a collection of gothic-looking cases that must be family heirlooms.

I scanned the crowd, wondering who would be waiting to collect us—to collect me. Would we be expected to move on en masse or whittled away, one by one, into our new respective families? Explosions of high-pitched sound erupted around me. A gaggle of girls. *Or is it a giggle?* My attention returned to the docks.

Should I be searching for a housekeeper, bundled off on errands for the day, or perhaps a lady-in-waiting? Would the estate be wealthy enough to have staff?

So little information had been shared with us before we departed France that we had created our own dream worlds where comfort and riches—and, of course, a handsome young man—awaited us.

No wealthy young men lingered at the dock—though I still didn't think it was worthy of the title—as gangplanks crashed onto heavy struts. Mud slopped along the banks in a steady stream. The river darkened in shadow as a steady line of impatient passengers formed, jostling around mountains of luggage.

My valise was much smaller, like fake sarcophagi

beginning to trend throughout the British nobility before I left France. The tiny coffers were supposed to house ancient holding mummies or the treasures of ancient Egypt when in reality they contained nothing more than the bodies of young urchins plucked from their own streets.

My own treasures were far less grandiose: several pairs of clean pantalettes and other *unmentionables*—a term Amy shared with me. What hang-ups the English had. I wondered how she would survive in the new world as a sharp sting on my neck reminded me of the whispers floating about the ship.

That our husbands were vehicles for the devil, never seen in society, seeking brides from abroad who would not have been subject to the more local rumor mill.

Or to have the chance to run away from it.

More common were the suspicions surrounding us, and our little wooden boxes. Several nosy passengers —women who knew nothing of courtesy sticking their plain faces into the occurrences of others—pestered us in the first few weeks. Some of the girls had become frustrated, upset, and so we had fabricated the rumor that *we* were the ones to be feared, shipped from our ruined homes to the colonies.

We hid in our cabins, laughing at the stupidity of the crowd, fueling the whisper of something aboard far worse than what might be waiting for us all in New Orleans: the dead subsisting on the living.

That we were, in fact, vampyre.

It was so laughable that we persisted in the rumor for all of a day. But as is the way with sensational news, the idea caught within the small community forced to exist together within wooden confines, igniting a small rush of panic throughout the ship. I snorted, stumbling on the hem of my dress as a passenger jostled me in his rush to meet the shore.

My box clutched in my arms, I placed each wary foot on the gangplank, chin raised as the nuns had taught me. Looking out at the crowd clustered around the jetty, I noticed a woman standing next to an empty cart. Not because she was active—quite the opposite. It was her complete lack of action that brought her out from the mob swarming around baggage and cargo as it was unloaded onto the muddy bank. Dressed in a plain, brown-belted tunic, she looked unassuming and bland in the chaotic flurry of color around us.

Trailed by a small line of chattering girls, I approached the woman, picking my way through the mud. Her eyes fixed on me, high cheekbones sucking in to give her a skeletal appearance, hair scraped in a severe bun. I smiled tentatively, my early training I'd had before my father lost his mind kicking in.

"Are you from Ursuline?" I asked, gritting my teeth at her stoic expression. "From the abbey—convent, I mean?" I smiled again, but she made no movement at all.

"She can't be the right one," a girl from the gaggle muttered over my shoulder.

"We should look around."

"Don't tell me we've been left behind!"

This last was accompanied by a high-pitched shriek. I closed my eyes as the sound echoed through my head, turning to shush the gaggle clustered behind me.

I turned back to the woman to find her nose inches to mine. Cold, colorless eyes peered into mine as though she delved into my own soul and found it empty. I squawked, retreating a step into the sticky mud underfoot. My worn soles didn't hold up to the task, my feet failing to find purchase in the mush of too many people milling about the crowded space. Slipping, I windmilled my arms for balance.

The ground shifted from *terra-firma* to *terra-slushius* beneath me. I closed my eyes, waiting to plunge into the slop but hands gripped my arms, steadying me. The ground stopped roiling, or maybe it was me. The girls hoisting me upright did their job to perfection. I smiled my gratitude at my two traveling companions.

We huddled together as the silent woman flipped open the back of her cart, motioning us into it. One by one, the girls climbed in. A small pile of wooden boxes filled the center as they found seats around the edges.

"Thank you," I murmured to the girls who were still clutching my arms.

None of us had moved, yet. An exchanged glance rippled through us. We moved together toward the cart, my hands stone cold in their warmer ones.

I released them with reluctance to shuffle on the dirty wooden flooring, my skirts swirling around my ankles, tattered lace catching on my heels. The woman retreated to the front of the cart, attending to her animal.

Twisting around, I sighted a figure I thought might be Amy, though no part of her was visible, ensconced beneath a heavy woolen coat even as the gnats stuck to my sweaty skin. Waving at the shrouded figure just in case, I took in the energy of the crowd: so much noise, chatter, and life, it reminded me of Paris as a child. If there were a place to see people at their best, it would be difficult to find a location better than this, I was certain.

Amy noticed my goodbye amongst the multitude gathered, shifting shadowed features into a wide grin as she rolled her eyes towards a young, handsome man, who leaned down to speak into her ear. He took her elbow, drawing her away and taking her attention with him.

A pang of loss struck my chest, even as I was nudged, and my attention returned to my own circumstances.

"Gissla. Gissy. *Gisselie*—"

"Gisella," I cut off the poor nun mangling my name.

She sent me a wilted smile and patted the step set below a foreboding woman dressed in a full habit.

The girl behind me stumbled, bumping me forward. I caught the rail to prevent myself from sprawling across the small interior of the cart. My land legs struggled against the combination of the solid ground I had yearned for versus the instability of a cart never meant to hold a swath of homesick travelers.

Finally, we were all seated, the cart bumping along a wide dirt path, peppered with potholes and stones. Chances were that my derrière wouldn't thank me come morning. I fervently hoped my mattress would be thick and minus any infestation, though watching clusters of gnats migrate from one girl to another, I had my doubts.

As the town receded, the countryside took over. Neither fields nor mountains spanned the landscape; instead, bogs and swampy trees, their moss-covered limbs dangling in the stagnant waters, overpopulated the flattened area.

I slapped at a large insect determined to drain my bodily fluids, and the girl next to me jumped.

She shrieked, pointing toward a river that wound its way around the bend. "What was that?"

"It was me, ninny. The sole thing to be afraid of is your own insensibilities." I snorted.

It wasn't as though my manners were required out in this mud-encrusted town. How would these girls, each born and bred in Paris, survive in this uncivilized land?

"No, *that!*"

This time, it was another girl who thrust a hand unceremoniously beneath my nose. I followed it to see a lump floating in the river. I opened my mouth to tell her not to be afraid of a decaying log when the lump in question launched itself from the putrid waters, revealing a prehistoric-looking creature, all slitted eyes and yellowed teeth.

My stomach roiled as the behemoth exploded from the water and snatched a bird from its perch on a vine above the waterline. The scaled beast sank back into the depths of the river, jaws clutched about its dead prize. The waters closed over its head, stilling in a deceptive vista of serenity.

My breath lodged in my throat. Not a sound broke the tentative silence of my traveling companions. Unwilling to be the least of us, I swallowed a scream as the cart rattled over a fragile bridge, praying it would hold our combined weight. We all peered over the side. Bubbles ruptured the surface, tiny ripples drifting away from the monster lurking beneath.

"It's *breathing*. Under the water," whispered the girl next to me. Shakes wracked her too-thin frame.

I nodded, unable to pry my jaw open lest I devolve into my own bout of hysterics, never to emerge sane again. Sobs echoed around me. More than one girl let her fear overcome her sensibilities. Determined not to join them—*yet*—I straightened, fluffing my skirts as though a predator at my side was nothing more than an everyday occurrence.

What fresh hell have we been sent to inhabit?

"What is it?"

The question fell from someone else's lips before I could ask, and I was glad for the opportunity not to betray my discomfort.

The nun offered a sliver of a smile from her perch.

"An alligator. Native to these parts. Fearsome monsters reside here, outside the waters, as well as within." She stared down at a group of girls huddled in the cart's far corner. Her smile remained as dead as her eyes, sending an ominous cloud rolling over all of us.

Perhaps the *les marais'* monsters were the lesser evil. I tried not to shiver, gripping my knees with whitened knuckles. The whole affair was laughable. We would be inside the abbey's confines and bored out of our minds within an hour.

The river and its horror would be left behind while we pretended to enjoy waiting for husbands who may or may not arrive to collect us. Worrying about some unknown future was both impractical and a useless waste of energy.

Yes, there were more things to occupy a woman's mind, more critical to her daily regime, especially a new one.

But no matter what dour thoughts I focused on to suppress my fanciful notions, a single, haunting realization remained lodged firmly within my mind.

The alligator was native to New Orleans. We were not.

Despite the stories we created on the ship about our journey, a coldness swept over me. What other creatures might we encounter in this wasted land of mud and myth?

What could be more terrifying than scales and a maw full of pointed teeth?

CHAPTER TWO

GISELLA

Though it was the height of day, the convent loomed above the meager path that led to its study doors. The details of the building seemed incomplete no matter how long I stared at the place. An impenetrable darkness blanketed everything its shadowy edges touched.

The moment we passed from the sunlight a chill drew over us, settling to the corners of our bodies, a weight of cold in the heart of the day.

One of the girls—who had never spoken during the journey at all to my knowledge—pulled back her bonnet to stare up at the three-storied building, as though reveling in the darkness.

While the other girls quivered in the shadow of God's house, this woman basked in it.

I repressed a shiver as we rattled across the cobblestones, my mouth clamped firmly around my tongue again. If I kept this up, I'd never manage to open the thing again.

"Do not be afraid," intoned the nun, and settled back into her permeating shroud of silence.

No small shadow will bow my back.

I reassured myself with the mantra despite the gooseflesh that pimpled my bare arms. The nun's gaze fixed on me, as though taking notice for the first time, and I could have sworn a hiss issued from between her lips.

"Afraid the archangel will take you, courtesan?"

I raised an eyebrow but refused to take her bait. *Courtesan, indeed.* Every one of the girls in the cart—herself included, I would wager, was a virgin, though we were sent to claim our marital beds.

I glanced toward the medieval building, so out of place, out of its time. Such establishments were commonplace in Paris, but here... The structure looked as though it had been hewn from the stone of the earth in some archaic nation and set afloat in this backwater community.

We followed the nuns to the front door of the abbey—plain and solid as I assessed on my first glance. Last of the line to slide down from the cart, I trailed the girls as they clustered together in a hushed, reverent silence. Each of us clutched our tiny caskets, nothing more than a line of orphans entering the gates of someone else's home that would never be ours.

Pausing at the threshold where shadowed tendrils clung to my boots, I placed my hand on the stone entryway. Even in the humid air, the building maintained its cold heart. No sliver of sunlight warmed its dank interior.

A shiver rippled along my spine, as though the air was changed with the presence of another, unseen. I turned, surveying the cleared drive, but the earth stood empty and alone. Shaking off the fancy as superstition I'd let the austere nun talk me into believing, I slipped beneath the stone lintel and stepped into the confines of the abbey.

My new home.

For now.

We climbed stairs to the third floor, following in the wake of our silent minder. Little furniture or decorations of any sort marked bare walls, their surfaces scarred and smoothed in an irregular pattern. One by one, each of us were ushered into small, sparsely decorated rooms with no more than an order to wait.

On what? The second coming, perhaps. My stomach grumbled. It had been a while since we last ate before the ship docked. That moment of stepping from the vessel seemed an age ago, though a few scant hours had passed since gnats nipped at my flesh, and I farewelled the friend I made during our passage.

Be safe. I hope he is good to you.

Whoever her *he* turned out to be. Yet another unknown in each of our futures, in *my* future.

Ignoring the residual swaying high in my belly, I focused on the present. Already I had spent too many hours fretting over things I couldn't control. My door was a stout fixture, the wood scarred from years of abuse from unknown prior occupants. The dull metal handle appeared to have been out of use for some time, matching my assessment of the entire third floor.

Why are they hiding us away up here like wraiths come to haunt the place forever?

More ridiculous notions. The abbey functioned on the lower floors, surely, though our tour hadn't included a glimpse into that aspect of the nun's life. Each room there would be taken up with a nun and her duties; they housed us above to prevent each orphan from inflicting change on their regular habit. That was all.

My feet began to ache, swelling within the worn leather. I looked around, surprised to find myself alone on the landing. The door leading from the stairs and the levels below closed with a thud that echoed along the narrow hallway. A halting screech added to the ricocheting sounds as a bolt was slung home on the other side.

Have the nuns heard the rumors we spread around the ship?

But how could they? We had arrived ourselves a few scant hours before.

With nothing else to distract me, I shot a glance in both directions along the empty hallway, pressed my hands to the heavy wood and pushed my door open.

The room—cell—was spartan, in keeping with the rest of the abbey. Walking beneath the lintel seemed a monumental effort, shedding my skin into a new life, though the mere barrier of a single step separated me from a bare hallway into an even more minimalist room.

A small table that held a bowl of thin, unidentifiable gruel sat next to a thin-framed bed. I placed my little box on the floor beside my mattress, hoping it was clean of earwigs and fleas. Those were rampant on the ship, and I'd taken pleasure in hunting down each critter and squishing it as a part of my pre-bedtime ritual.

I spooned the heavily spiced soup into my mouth. The lumps hid whatever the true flavor was, and I suspected I should be thankful for that. As the sun sank below the horizon through a small glassed, barred window, shadows lengthened across the room. Given no candle, I huddled beneath my thin blanket and tried not to think of the man who would collect me at dawn.

As it was, I didn't have to wait that long.

Wrapped in a threadbare, smoky-scented cloak, I got married to a nun. Or rather, married by proxy. A nun whisked me from my room with a hiss, bundling me and my meager possessions down the stairs to the ground floor where I waited alone in a shroud of darkness.

At the foot of the drive stood a carriage, a silhouette in the moonless night. The Abbess—noteworthy in her pristine robes at an indecent hour—performed the ceremony in a spate of Latin she rattled off while my brain wondered how on earth things could possibly be so different in this backward country.

The only words I recognized were my own, and my husband's name.

Sebastian Lammert Aguillard.

I rolled his name—now my own—around in my head, memorizing it, testing it to see how our names sounded together. Gisella Marie Aguillard. It didn't sound too bad, and Sebastian was a clean name on its own. I imagined a rotund man with a tanned face from the deadly bayou's blistering sun, perhaps a donkey or a cart in the background.

Why go to such lengths to maintain secrecy?

I had no doubt that this midnight ceremony conducted in the quiet hours hidden away from any eyes whatsoever outside of its circle was of a covert nature.

While I had no objection in being married by a woman—to ostensibly yet another woman—I was certain Rome would have plenty to say about it. My father, too. But he'd given those rights away when he sold me to the King of France's pithy whim.

The ceremony concluded, the nun I'd married faceless in the dark of night pressed a paper-thin hand to my forehead, whispering a frantic blessing over me before I was hastened into the waiting carriage at the foot of the abbey's drive.

Such a short time. A few hours and already I miss

the peace of my threadbare room, away from the sisters who without whom I was suddenly bereft.

Better the devil you know...

My future merged with the present until I was left in a void between my past life and my future fate, alone and exposed in a midnight purgatory. Swallowing my fear where it joined uncertainty somewhere in the depths of my stomach, I studied the carriage before me.

Covered in the shadow of night, there was no detail, no coat of arms visible on the door. The door opened silently, well oiled. The driver, swathed in a heavy cloak of darkness, stared down at me from his high perch. Something about him seemed...wrong. I could see him, but not sense him, as though he were a painting and not really there at all. I nodded briskly, unwilling to trust my voice, and stepped into the void within.

A dark velvet covered the bench cushions as I settled into the interior. Without waiting for a rap of knuckles or a shouted order, the carriage lurched forward as soon as I had seated myself.

I clutched my little box against my chest until my skin ached, the bumpy road away from the abbey no better than the one from the docks. I hoped it would be a shorter trip, but my midnight rousing stilled with the miles of countryside passing by that I couldn't see. Soon enough, my eyes grew bleary, and I closed them, seeking the silence of sleep.

When the driver stopped for relief, I stowed the

casket beneath my seat, clamping my boots over it for the last part of our journey, however long it might be. Something heavy rolled against my fingers as I fidgeted with the box. A quick rap on the door startled me—he was much faster than I assumed.

"Madame." A shuffling noise accompanied his fist, rapping on the roof of the carriage. "When you're ready." His voice was rough, carrying the edge of midnight secrets in it.

A frisson ran over my skin at his tone. I tugged my cloak about my body, as though it would be anything but a poor defense if the man proved untrustworthy. My mind disagreed; arguing its case that the man would protect me as efficiently as he towed me from one destination to the next in the midst of night should some unfortunate circumstance befall our voyage.

"Ready," I called out, extracting what looked like an exceptional bottle of *beaujolais*. I fiddled with the neck until a corkscrew rolled timely onto my boot. *When in need...* Smiling at my own half-formed humor, I inserted the thing with little finesse and hoped the coachman wouldn't hit any bumps in the interim.

Freed of its enclosure, the heady scent of berries and ash filled the small cabin. Glinting in the small light of the coach lamps, I made out the label, *Sister's Landing*. A squat building was etched above the variety.

Yet another abbey.

I determined never to go there.

The bottle kept me company over many miles of

rough terrain, and when we arrived at our destination, the ground was decidedly unstable. I rose on wobbly legs, unsure if the air had infected the wine, or if New Orleans had infected *me*. I teetered on my boots, muttering under my breath about sleepy feet and pitched unceremoniously forward.

The coachman caught me as I toppled from the step to what appeared to be several paces to the ground. Large, calloused hands gripped my body until I seemed impossibly fragile before his bulk. I gasped as his thick arm wound around my waist, tugging me back against his body.

His frame was hard, like granite. Leaning back into him was nothing like innocent forays with the youths of my limited debut; this man was colder than a gravestone, contained within the same stillness. I spun around, but his gloved hands cinched my waist, offering no release.

A jolt passed through my body, my core clenched as he leaned into me, his cool breath wreaking havoc on my senses. That same sense of nothingness despite the evidence my body offered niggled at me.

But the man's presence... God above. Had he given me an order, I would have followed it without question. Authority exuded from him, and my body reacted to his silent demand, softening in his grasp.

"I am not, I mustn't—" I couldn't force the right words past my lips beneath his midnight gaze. His eyes were fathomless in the depths of the night. As the false dawn approached, he squeezed my waist as though testing my mettle. Sensation zinged through me at the contact, while my mind screamed at me to *move*. But I didn't want to move. I whimpered and attempted to cover the moment of weakness with an unladylike cough. "Let me down," I hissed. My breath puffed between the bared flesh of his neck and my cheek. "This *cannot happen*."

I made it a statement; no *sir* as the English had their habit. Every word pushed against some insatiable desire to give into this man. But we were no longer in England, or France, or Europe.

Instead, I had been dunked into this edge of primordial sludge and told to make a life of it.

Lost in my reflections, I realized the coachman still had a hold of me as I reached back to collect my box. I froze, repressing the urge to squeal—for what an igno-minious noise that would be—and waited for him to remove his hands, as requested.

As I demanded.

Donning defiance as my shield, I tilted my head back and stared haughtily down my nose; a habit picked up from a previous abbey and a past life I shucked in return for humid air and biting insects.

"Only if you do not wish it." His reply to my demand brushed over the nape of my neck in a brief caress.

I shivered. His counteroffer had a finality to it as he swept inside, his thick cloak swirling around his shoulders.

Then the contact was gone, and a whisper of cold air remained in the wake of his touch.

Another footman rushed forward to attend me. I stood inert, wondering what just happened, mulling over his words.

Only if you do not wish it.

CHAPTER THREE

SEBASTIAN

My new wife shied away from me like a skittish mare, but the defiance in her eyes defined her. Drew me to her, until I came within an inch of throwing off my cloak and unmasking myself before her. Claim her there on the drive, be damned what any of my staff thought, or expected. This woman was *mine*.

In every way.

Not that she would forgive me for such an act, an intrusion without her permission, no matter how much I craved her the moment my dead skin touched hers. Fragile she might appear and feel beneath my hands, but her eyes flashed with a fierce independence far more attractive than any other quality she might possess.

The taste of her lingered in the night air, a flavor of innocence tainted already with the evils of this place.

Of myself, and the evils I carried with me across oceans, over unnatural lifetimes.

Cursing myself as a fantastical fool, I tossed the reins to the stableboy waiting in the shadows. My eyes weren't the only ones that had followed my wife's flight. I clipped the boy gently across the back of the head, a not-so-subtle reminder of his place, and mine.

The house's silhouette lengthened with the night as I paced through the lower halls, ignoring the new presence above me while Charleton escorted her to her rooms. I couldn't shake the feel of her where she clung to my tarnished soul, aching to rip him away from her and terrorize her in the bedroom set aside for her use. It wasn't likely that we would spend that many hours together, considering my nocturnal custom, unless she was prepared to flip not only her French lower nobility life for me, but her sleeping habits too. I probed her mind gently, the faint scent of night jasmine and naivety lingering though we were a floor apart.

The corner of my lip curled. A virgin, as promised. How...sweet. I could have taken one of the courtesans offered, their souls already shredded, but some part of me wanted to have a slice of purity in this life, if only for a short period. My conversation with my local stone mason echoed through my mind.

"You'll outlive her by an eon. Ten, a hundred. Will your immortal soul deal with her death after a lifetime of regrets?" His knowing eyes settled on mine, the sort of broken soul he spoke of reflected intimately there.

At the time it was all too easy to laugh off his romanticized notion. Now, I wondered there wasn't more truth in his wisdom.

Gisella's sharp opinions echoed inside my mind for a brief moment as she berated the valet silently before they flittered away, and I lost the connection. I smiled despite the pain clenching my chest, wishing it was air I breathed, and not her life I craved.

Desperation clawed at me to reclaim her, but now wasn't the time to intrude further than I already had on her singular night of peace before she was thrown headfirst into my world. There would be time. An eternity of nothingness in which to discover her.

A dry laugh, less a polite sound than something from the bowels of hell itself, ripped from my throat. But even my solitary hours weren't to be my own.

"My lord. You requested me upon your return."

I stared across the small room I didn't recall entering at the slip of a girl who stood before me, her hands clasped at waist height. "How old are you?"

"Six and ten. My lord," she added. Her voice wobbled, though she made a valiant effort to keep it firm.

I swatted a hand at her. "I don't remember you. Send me Elvira, or one of the girls I often use, please."

I turned away, not watching her leave, and focused on the extra presence upstairs, near my rooms. *Sixteen.* For fuck's sake. Charlton knew better. She might be considered an adult of serviceable age here or in

France, but I refused to destroy an innocent girl on a whim because I couldn't touch my wife.

My wife.

A depraved smile curled my lips. The girl squeaked, but my efforts weren't for her. Gisella was the only innocent I wanted to ruin.

Going up her rooms tonight was the worst of plans. My hunger bore a hole in my gut that was never satisfied no matter how much I drank, like an addict with too many empty bottles seeking that next, and least effective, hit.

Perhaps that's what Gisella would be for me. My newest addiction to cover the yawning void inside me where a soul once resided. Before a sorceress decided to experiment on a man who found beauty and worshipped that instead of understanding the creature it hid within.

That catastrophe was so long ago I barely remembered my humanity, and the ending of it the birthing into my monstrous side I'd use to rip every fraction of her innocence away.

Whether she wanted it or not.

"Sebastian."

This time the voice was older, stained with a suggestive lilt. Any other night I would have welcomed the distraction, but tonight was a marking point for change.

I waved a hand without looking at her. "Elvira. Thank you for coming." I kept my voice formal, my stance stiff. "I am hungry. Push your hair back."

She didn't step forward as I expected. "And my clothes?"

Still the lilt remained despite the disassociation in my stance. *These humans never learn.*

I'd been one, once, and look how that pitiful existence ended. Or rather, how it didn't end. Never would. The irony tore a ruined laugh from my throat, and she took a step back, her seductive expression turning wary.

"Your clothes may stay where they are, on your form. I married tonight. I need to eat, and that is all." I beckoned her, staring at a point above her head.

I didn't need to persuade her to do what I wanted, or I'd risk warping her mind.

But I did take the time to brush my thoughts against Gisella's and found her wandering the halls where she shouldn't be. I smiled at the thought of discovering her in the darkest corners, wrapping my hands around her slim waist and pulling her into the shadows to play. My cock hardened, and Elvira perked up.

"So I am food?"

I didn't need to look at her to see the pout of her generous lips reflected in her eyes, the way her lips curved up in temptation.

Fucking insatiable mortals don't understand hunger.

However, it wasn't the pretty serving girl that roiled my blood with need but the image of my wife in my arms, her head tipped back, soft, wine-stained lips pulsing with life that left me hard and straining against the fabric of my breeches.

"You are nothing more than a meal. Tonight is your last shift. After this you are free." My command whiplashed through the silent lower floor so close to the servant's quarters. I was certain they would hear our tiff, less of a lover's quarrel than a master and employee's impersonal dispute over time and pay, though I doubted she saw it that way. A job, and service rendered.

Good. Then they'll understand my needs.

"My lord." Elvira dropped to her knees at my feet, fretting like a mouse without a house.

My lips curled cruelly. "Head back. Like a good girl."

Her whimper at my instruction, usually said in private when we were both divested of clothing, and me buried to the hilt inside her, was meaningless, and cold.

Heartless, like me.

I will tear her apart.

And she will love me for it.

The entire time I feasted I thought of Gisella. Her pale flesh torn apart beneath my hands, her bones fragile, brittle. Her life beating frantically against my tongue as I took her to the edge again and again.

And when I was done, a shell of a woman was left, one I barely recognized as my once lover, no longer my servant.

"She must leave this house tonight," I murmured to

the younger sister who could have taken her place earlier. Wide, white eyes stared at me, written with the fresh horror of a thousand nightmares yet to be had. "You, too. Charleton will compensate you both handsomely. Leave this place," I repeated, stalking to the mineral rock pools the house was built over, needing to cleanse myself.

Purify, before I touched her.

I had a wife to terrorize.

CHAPTER FOUR

GISELLA

My heart thundering in my chest in a delayed response after I left the carriage and the strange shadow man behind, I followed the tall valet who carried my tiny casket that contained my scant belongings to my room.

Suite was more appropriate.

I barely saw the house or its halls, stumbling over my own feet in my haste to keep up with the speedy man, but I saw plenty of my own room, turning circles on the plush, patterned carpets, standing in the starlight that filtered through the arched windows.

My new home was a tower room. Bring in the dragon if you will, sir. Perhaps a moat to complete the picture. My accomplice scurried off, leaving me alone in my second new home on the same day.

Married to a nun, swept away to a castle home.

Even I could see that the building, though common in my homeland, was out of place in this new world. All flat sands and rivers and archaic reptilian nightmares...my new home looked so out of place I struggled to understand how my husband had built the place unless by pure force of will alone.

Clearly, I'd hit the realm of fantastical notions. That thought could go right back into my casket, along with the intense coachman with his hungry eyes. I shivered, stepping outside my door and venturing a short distance along the hallway, but the shadows beckoned, and I darted back into my room, slamming the door shut and pressing my back to its unyielding surface.

I'd wake in the morning, still in my old room in my father's house half a world away to discover this fairytale was all but a dream.

If it could be true.

I pushed away from the door, turning about the room too fast. The wine and my spinning took the mass of color with it, leaving me heady and swaying. I collapsed onto the bed, missing the pillows by a good measure. My aim didn't matter; the mattress was enormous. I sank into its soft comfort, letting its plush surface curve around my weary body.

Too tired—or too drunk—to bother taking off my boots, I fell asleep in the same tattered dress I'd traveled across oceans to marry a man I hadn't met yet.

My fleeting dreams were filled with shadows, midnight eyes in the face of a man I couldn't see, and illicit kisses that faded as I awoke but craved all the same.

Daybreak, and breakfast, arrived far too early for my disposition; drapes were drawn aside with a combination of sighs and exclamations. Sighs from the army of maids who invaded my serene brand of darkness— such a happy plane to exist on a self-induced blue devil—and exclamations from me when sunlight burned my eyes. I rolled in my sheets, drowning in my pillow and using my sleep-matted hair as a barrier. If the staff were so enthused, couldn't they visit another member of the household?

I burrowed deeper, swearing softly in my native tongue. A tap to my shoulder told me it was time to face the day. As gracefully as possible, I turned my rat's nest of a head, certain it was nothing less, to the maid who proffered a pot of coffee beneath my nose.

"*Merci*," I mumbled, attempting to sweep a tangle of frizzy knots from my face.

She gave me a bright smile and a bobbed curtsy. I watched the pot with no little trepidation. Being scalded on the morning I was to meet my new husband was *not* how I intended to spend my first day in a new life.

The young girl—she could surely be no more than six and ten, two younger than myself, perhaps— poured the coffee deftly into a porcelain cup decorated with minuscule cornflower blue patterns. It reminded me so much of the set *Maman* had kept for special occasions that my stomach lurched, accompanied by a prickling around the corners of my eyes.

I blinked rapidly, trying to disguise the panic rising inside me, and failed miserably if the look on the girl's face was anything to judge by.

"What—" I swallowed with a dry throat, trying to form words. More coffee was offered beneath my nose, and I took a grateful sip. I nodded my thanks. "What's your name?"

"Minette, madame." Though her voice was clear and high, it was horribly mangled by the hideous accent I'd encountered on the docks.

Realizing that this was, in fact, the way they spoke here, I resolved to teach my maid—*Minette* —conversational French, at least.

"Well, Minette," I enunciated each word as an example, but quickly, lest she assumed I thought her a simpleton, "Thank you for greeting the morning with me. Am I not to break my fast with—" I stumbled—*what was I supposed to call him?* "Ah, the Master of the House?"

Minette's eyes widened, and she leaned forward, checking over her shoulder. I sighed; if this was their idea of intrigue, I was in for a very boring life. My heart panged at the mere memory of all that Paris encompassed that slipped away with every new moment I experienced in the new world.

"Oh no, madame," she whispered, clutching the

breakfast tray. Its contents rattled a little, and I was surprised to see her hands were shaking. "The master won't be down until well into the evening. After the sun sets." She gave me a sideways glance, fussed with the tray until she was satisfied it was set up correctly, and vacated the room without another word.

I stared into my bowl of congealed mess. Wilted berries swam in a scarlet pool of their own juices. The coffee that whisked my attention away a moment before turned nauseating in my stomach. I pushed the tray aside, extracting the coffee, and edged into the morning sunlight. My window overlooked the gardens, and a swampy forest beyond, dark and foreboding even in the morning light. There wasn't another building in sight. Not a stable, nor a cottage.

Where was the plantation? We were all meant to be plantation owners' wives, or so we'd been told. What other lies had we been fed? My throat tightened, restricting my breath in a noose-like style of my own making.

I was a continent away from everything I understood, in a place so totally unknown to me. Was I even in the right place? And who the hell had I married? In the space of a single night, I'd become the property of a man I'd never met.

"*Sacre bleu*," I whispered.

I craned around the edge of my balcony, but was welcomed with the darkness we traveled through in the carriage and beyond, the bogs—pardon me, bayou, or so Amy had told me. Such a pretty name for a parasite-infested swamp housing ancient predators.

I slapped at one of the little insects, fat and healthy as it sucked on my arm. It exploded with the impact, splattering my skin in a stain that refused to budge. I swiped the gruesome mess away with the hem of my dress, ignoring the stain in both skin and skirt. Everything here seemed either intent on eating me or came from a myth that said they would.

My thoughts turned to my husband. *Didn't show himself until after dark?* What a lazy man. And missing the best parts of the day, I groused, watching the sun rise. Light filtered over the odd trees below, giving it a sheen of life. I smiled, glad I could still appreciate the beauty of the sunrise, despite my own exhaustion.

My mind clicked back to my time on the ship with the other *filles a la cassette*, and the rumors we had encouraged. Was it possible the staff believed my husband to be a creature of the night?

I swallowed at the thought, tracing the landscape with my gaze alone as if seeking proof of the insidious idea, or assurance that I was as silly as the gaggle of girls I left behind at the convent. My gaze drifted across the greenery blooming amongst cultured gardens and wilderness beyond the heavy gray stone of the house. The foliage gave the impression of life, though the canopy protected whatever secrets lay beneath.

If the servants believed the Master to be a vampyre, I would struggle to find any sort of social life here, at all. That gave me pause. I dressed quickly in the pale peach gown the maid had laid out, grateful its simple ties allowed me the ability to dress myself. I knew I'd have to give that up at some point, but for today, I sent up a simple prayer of gratitude.

Brushing my own hair—a task the other Casket girls and I used to swap—felt strange, an almost lonely endeavor. Determined not to focus on the negative connotations, I took it instead as a foray into the independence of my new life in this new-to-me world. A smile bloomed across my face, and I headed for the door to my room with a lighter step.

Tying my blue sash to the door handle so I could find it again, I looked down the hall, which seemed to disappear into the darkness. *This land is full of unearthly shadows.* And...fanciful again. Fanciful, fanciful. It was my favorite word, one Amy taught me, her rose and pale skin glowing even within the ship's lightless bowels.

Opposite my room stood a pair of doors, though I dared not open them in the event of waking said slumbering husband and finding an ogre in his place. Instead, I headed to the other end of the hall where an open staircase led to the lower floor—where I had entered last night, perhaps.

But the darkness beyond called to me.

The light flickered in brief spats along the walls. I took a hesitant step into the dim passage, my path lightened as I pushed forward, straining my eyes though I couldn't see much more than a dozen feet in front of my face. Still, I didn't let a little thing like lack of vision deter me. I was determined to make the most of my discovery time, free without servants clamoring household rules at me.

Finding my way through the enormous house—it missed out on castle status by perhaps a foot—was an interesting journey. Similar to my home, my *father's* home, seeing as it hadn't been *mine* in any aspect of the word for years, many of the rooms were furnished, but appeared not to be in use. Though each new door displayed an impeccably kept room, from the lack of any sort of warmth or feel, most hadn't seen company for many years, or perhaps never.

A façade of an enormous, out of place manor house, and an absentee master. It was the stuff that heralded fairy stories from my own country. If I turned widdershins three times around the gardens, perhaps the fêtes would whisk me away to yet another land, another life. Another Amy term I learned on board the ship.

So fanciful.

Servants galore passed me, bobbing their white caps with a slurred *madame*—I would never get used to their accent but promised myself to make the most of educating them as best I could as the mistress of the house. Another turn on a sharp corner, and I found myself in the same corridor I'd started in, staring at my own bedroom door. My blue sash dangled from the handle, exactly as I had left it. It moved slightly, though there was no breeze.

A breath brushed my nape, bringing my mind

forcibly back to the erotic dreams I suffered through, their intimate, ghostly caresses, tossing me in my sleep to the thought that someone watched me in my room.

But when I woke, the dawn greeted me, bright and clean of any other presence. No phantom presence hung in my tower room, apart from the maid with her endless supply of happiness and food.

And yet, the same presence stood behind me now, in my wakeful moments.

Another breath, the barest caress on my skin meant my dreams were one thing, my reality another. In the lonely halls of a great house in the midst of nowhere, I wasn't alone.

CHAPTER FIVE

GISELLA

"Excuse me." A soft, deep voice sent a shiver rippling over me, caressing my collarbone.

My phantom.

I spun on my heel, determined not to shriek. He was only a man, after all.

But it wasn't just *a* man, but *the* man. The coachman from last night. Midnight eyes surveyed me, the barest hint of humor lurking in their shadows.

Was he...laughing at me?

"Good morning," I croaked, fervently wishing my voice would work as expected when called upon.

I aimed for an imperious look but when my gaze swept over him my intentions crumbled as I gawked at the man, seeing his face in full for the first time.

Deep red lips dominated a swarthy complexion framed with lustrous, thick hair, highlighted by a sheen of rare obsidian. I watched his lips move as he spoke, entranced. Then I realized he *had* spoken, and I hadn't heard a word.

"I'm sorry." I blinked at him. "What did you say?"

His eyes hooded, he gazed back at me. "I hope that you enjoy your...stay, madame."

"I'm sure I will."

While my brain screamed that I would do no such thing, I could do nothing but stare as my hand lifted of its own accord, apparently. He bowed low over my fingers, and I could have sworn he kissed my hand, a flicker of sensation zinging over my skin though there remained a distance between my flesh and his. His eyes lifted to capture mine again.

My body reacted as though I were too close to a blazing bonfire, both drawn to his beauty and alarmed by his intensity. Heat pooled low between my thighs, my breasts aching with the need for *more*.

I stepped toward him as though he had asked it of me, intent on studying his face further when he straightened. The sharp gesture froze me where I stood. The lightest smile graced the corners of his lips. Inclining his head, he watched me a second longer and strode away. The hall's incessant darkness swallowed him until he might never have been there at all.

I stood still, life and the household's manic pace resuming as a sudden onslaught of servants bustled around me. Blinking once more into the darkened end of the hall, I berated myself for the notions that ran about in my head, warding them away, and headed in the opposite direction.

At the top of the stairs, a suited manservant greeted me.

"You would like a tour, madame?"

"I'm not a madame," I protested, though some part of my brain reminded me I had been married last night, and might, in fact, be madam of this house. I blinked wide eyes at the footman—*butler?*—no doubt appearing as stupid as he expected me to be.

To my surprise, he placed a kind hand on my arm.

"You are welcome here. Please, allow me to show you your new home."

His touch lightened, hesitant. I wondered again at the rules of this place, the social etiquette of a mismatched patchwork quilt. Not wishing to be impolite, I gestured with my other hand.

"Lead on...?" I let my sentence hang.

"Charleton, madame." He bowed low, dropping his hand as though recognizing the impropriety.

Despite the lapse, I smiled. Charleton was the first true connection I'd found in this place, other than with my maid, and I refused to let the small social aspect evade me.

The staircase descended in a broad arc that curved around a central pillar, wide enough for ten men to stand abreast across it. "Down here, you will find the dining room and the library. Though there is a small library on your floor you might prefer," he added.

"Oh?" I pressed my slipper into the scarlet carpet.

The sole sank deeply, but when I turned to look back, there was no trace of our passing.

Heavy, brocade drapes covered every window, removing sunlight from the house's interior in its entirety. Wall sconces lit the staircase and lower floors in a kaleidoscope of flickering shadows and dancing flames. Had I not looked out my own small balconette, I would never have known what time of day it was— or if it was day, at all.

"I believe his Lordship has stocked the room with as many French books as possible. Some classics, some more...risqué." His lip curled on the word *French*, and by the time he had finished, white teeth glistened between pale lips.

I studied the man. Maybe a few years past his prime, his otherwise sallow skin glowed in the house's unnatural light.

"Could we open the curtains, perhaps?" I smiled at the pasty man, who had a European look. I wondered when he had emigrated.

Charleton jumped as though I had shoved a hot poker up his trouser leg. "The—the light is very bright here, my lady... you must understand, we must save the portraits—the ark—the art!" Managing to enunciate his excuse, he coughed, stumbling over his words. "Yes, the artwork. We must protect it always. From fading," he added, unconvincingly.

I frowned at bare walls, tracking my eyes along the corridor for anything that would require *saving*.

An iron hand pressed in the center of my back

propelled me along, and we turned into an enormous space. Black and white square tiles filled the floor more suited to Paris than this strange land I still didn't understand. Pillars were decorated with silver vines that crept along tall columns to meet the high ceiling. A dark fresco was painted there, a scene of hunting and firelight and death.

In the middle of the painting, a chandelier half the width of the room descended, tiny crystals shattering light across the floor from its great height, giving me the impression I walked across an expanse of stars.

"The ballroom."

I nodded, turning in a circle with my mouth hanging open. I didn't care if I drooled; it was the most beautiful room I'd ever seen.

"It's—it's—" Apparently, I'd caught Charleton's stutter. The man was contagious.

"Magnificent." A soft, deep voice swept across the room, wrapping around me like a chilled wind and warm fire at once.

Charleton's eyes widened. He bowed, backing from the room, his gaze lowered to the floor.

I turned in circles again, looking over my shoulder in every direction, but I was the sole occupant in the room. Spinning around, my mouth opened to call out for—anyone, really, I came face to face with a man who stood motionless inches from me.

I jerked, stumbling as a whimper left my lips. I hated the moment the sound escaped, but that didn't appear to deter my stalker. He didn't move, but opted to watch me with those same midnight dark eyes that filled his perfect, angular face.

Everyone here is too beautiful for their own good.

I huffed inside my head as I righted myself, taking in his pointed collared shirt, bright beneath slim lines of a black coat and breeches. A shadow brushed his chin, as though he hadn't shaved in a day or more.

The same face that had accosted me earlier; the same face of the coachman from the evening before, now dressed as though he owned the place.

As the penny dropped to an empty purse, I realized that he did.

Surely, this was my husband.

Sebastian.

"My lord, I—"

"Magnificent," he murmured again, the words swirling around me, stepping forward. His eyes never left me, and I knew he wasn't talking about the ballroom anymore. "I am not your lord."

"Oh."

Eloquence left me. My mind a total blank, I decided it must have left its residence, too.

"Sebastian." My own manners deserted me as the butler's had earlier.

I expected a proffered hand, mine already grasping in response, but there was nothing. I jerked my fingers back, confused. My heart beat faster, thrumming in my ears. A tingle itched at my skin again at his proximity. Should I run and hide from this man? Even at this simple level of engagement, he reminded me of the alligator breathing beneath the water, waiting.

Everything about this place was nothing I'd ever encountered before.

Is all of the new world like this?

If it were, then they were an odd offshoot of the British, having strayed so far from the proverbial tree.

"And you— this is your place?" I asked, my mind still finding its feet.

"This is my home." The final word came out guttural and twisted.

Why did the owner of a mini-castle drive his own carriage to collect me yesterday but not introduce himself?

Why did I not marry this man, instead of a nun?

He'd been there, on the coach. Watching. Waiting, like now.

None of my questions made it as far as my lips. My brain jammed, attempting to process too many ideas at once.

"Why did you not say who you were last night?" My brain finally caught up with my situation to ask a relevant question.

See? Not fanciful.

"I did not want to frighten you." His words were a soft admission, not quite an apology.

My husband studied me frankly, and I returned the favor, taking in his height, the substantial width of his chest and shoulders. Again, the diminutive feeling swept over me, his presence bigger than the man himself.

I wasn't alone in my study. Done with my face, his gaze detoured along my frame. I refused the urge to clench my fists beneath his surveillance. As his gaze rose back to my face, his coal eyes darkened. An unfamiliar heat flushed my cheeks.

"You are my husband." I raised my chin, determined to maintain some semblance of control.

"Yes," he almost hissed the word, stepping forward into my space, covering the short distance in a graceful stride. One moment, he was away from me; the next, he stood too close.

I swallowed, planting my feet so I couldn't retreat, but started as his hand wound around my elbow. His touch was cool, but it was his eyes that sent a riot of shivers over my skin.

Hooded and dark, they promised nights of dark sin, as though he would devour me, never allow me to see the light of day once more. Sebastian wound me into him, bit by bit, until a layer of thin material separated us.

It was like being next to a carved statue; nothing emanated from him. No heat, no life, but at the same time, the huge man was imposing beyond belief. His presence emanated from a distance but up close, he was a void against the stark beauty of the room.

But his eyes—those were alive with a shadowy passion. Shivers crossed my skin again, and this time it had nothing to do with his touch. His hand dropping, he retreated. Those midnight dark eyes never leaving me, he dipped in a bow, lips parting as though about to speak.

That same void, a sense of all and nothingness returned, freezing time itself. With a brisk nod, he turned, disappearing in a blur of movement.

My feet carried me to the edge of the large room as they chased him of their own accord. When I reached the doorway, I was alone.

I blinked, wondering what I had missed, and what in all of Dante's circles just happened.

For a house as populated and large as my new home, no one was around when I searched. Charleton had disappeared into the depths of the house, it appeared. Retracing my steps ended up being the best thing I could do. Lost in a myriad of hallways, I discovered studies and sitting rooms, bed chambers enough to house a hundred guests, and a small salon.

Finally, I ended up in a long portrait gallery. Lined with the same, heavy carpet that filled most of the house, it was a muted, quiet hall. Thick floor to ceiling drapes covered an entire section at one end of the hall.

The row of paintings appeared to be of the same man, over and over, in different clothes. The evolution of Sebastian's forefathers was like watching the passing of the ages in a static form. Apparently, there was a strong family resemblance in Sebastian's line. I shook my head. *Not a lord.* I didn't even know his proper title.

None of the portraits had a name plaque, but the fashions gave me an idea of the era each one had been painted in—perhaps a one-hundred-year gap between each. Not a single window decorated this hall—*protect the artworks, my panniers.*

Charleton was conspicuously absent in my journey.

Three more drawing rooms, two sitting rooms, and a library later, I was still alone in the house. Or, so it seemed. Every time I entered a room, I could have sworn a person sat in one of the chairs, or beside the fireplace.

But when I looked closer, my phantoms proved to be no more than a play in the flickering light from the sconces that dominated every wall space. Dancing shadows in my periphery remained the lone artwork on the walls of this barren place. However luxuriously fitted, the building lacked something. Life, I supposed, looking around for the servants who had overpopulated the rooms this morning and were now conspicuous in their absence.

A small pile of books sat on a lone desk. Far from a cluttered space, the cherrywood furniture sat back against the far end of the room, beneath midnight blue curtains that cast the room in a cool, masculine light. I strode across the space, determined to see sunlight, and wrenched the curtains apart.

A blank wall stared back at me.

I swallowed, the wall looming over me as if I were prey. My hip hit the edge of the desk. With a soft croak,

I moved around it, gathering the books on top as though to prove that they, at least, were real, and backed from the room, straight into a soft, warm body.

"I'm so sorry!"

I turned, hands grasping for purchase on the door-frame. The books thumped onto the floor. A small, bird-like maid swayed before me. Pasty, and looking as though she was about to retch, she sank to the floor. My hands wrapped around her head, scraping the carpet as they bore her weight to the floor.

"Charleton!" I screeched over the maid's head, her cap tumbling from her hair as I straightened her on the floor with careful hands, praying the man had omnipotent qualities. "Help me!"

The young woman's eyelids fluttered over closed eyes, red staining her starched collar. I wrenched at the edge of my skirts, pressing the torn fabric to her neck. Brushing away hair, I saw a thin line across her neck, weeping bright scarlet beads onto her clothes.

Holding material bunched into my hand, I yelled for Charleton again, but not before I saw a collection of similar thin, white lines decorating the other side of her neck.

Charleton appeared beside me, lifting the woman into his arms.

"I'll take her, madame," he dismissed me.

My skin prickled with unspent rage, fear and a heady dose of confusion.

"Press something to her neck," I snapped, refusing to release the maid. "She's bleeding. And if she is part of this household, then she is mine to look after." I glared at the manservant over the maid's small frame. A moment of stillness, then he gave a jerk of his chin, motioning to her things on the floor where she had collapsed.

"If you would, please..." He glanced down at the still form in his arms, gripping her with aged, white-knuckled hands. "Follow me."

I nodded silently, collecting her tools.

The servant's quarters were as bland and functional as a room could be. The distinct opposite to the luxury in the rest of Sebastian's house, I wondered that we didn't see more revolts between servant and master. Or perhaps they protested in other, more silent forms where a wary eye would strain to notice.

Stark, unadorned rooms, tiled floors and colored walls filled the servant's quarters. Did anyone *live* in this place? Charleton placed the maid onto a sagging bed, its slim mattress hanging low in the middle, a flat pillow stacked at one end.

He took bandages and a vial of clear liquid from a box on the floor, reminding me of the casket I carried across the seas. I raised a hand, ready to object as he began to treat her himself until I saw the steadiness of his hands, the way he touched her. A faint smile tickled the corners of my lips; love hadn't forsaken this unusual place, yet.

Finally, the tall, thin man rose. Exhaustion etched his features. I drew him from the tiny room—little more than the cell I'd been placed in at the abbey—and closed the door behind us.

"Does she do it often?" I asked, softly.

Charleton started. "What?"

I hadn't believed he could be any pastier, but at the rate blood drained from his face, he would become a cadaver himself soon enough.

"She hurts herself, yes?"

He stared at me for a long moment, as though ready to argue with me. Thin lips pursed, he nodded. "She—hurts."

That's not the same thing.

But it would have to do.

"How long have you looked after her like this?" I asked. "You're quite fond of her."

"No! I—" he cut himself off.

"No?" I raised an eyebrow.

"Well, yes...It's been a long time since we had a lady in the house," he said, managing to meet my eyes, though he bobbed his gaze back to the floor soon after. "A long time."

His words held an undercurrent I couldn't decipher. I tucked the information away to look at later.

"Madame." My maid, Minette who had introduced herself during her flurry earlier, her words sinking in slowly throughout the day, appeared by my elbow with a glass of water. "Food will be brought up to your rooms."

I thought of my bedroom—enormous, luxurious, and empty.

"Might I have lunch with you?"

Minette's eyes widened, flicking between Charleton and myself.

I hastened to reassure her. "I don't mind who I eat with. I've been on board a ship, stuffed into cabins for months and here—here, I am so lonely," I finished softly, aghast at the quiet truth of my words.

Not even one full day.

Minette nodded, letting me follow her through the warrenlike halls in her preparations. Despite her chatty nature, she was silent through lunch, a collection of small meals that might have been leftovers from the day before. Each held a French flourish, a kind reminder that this new home and my old had some connection other than me.

I closed my eyes, sitting back in the low armchair. When Minette had been hesitant to set the large dining table, I suggested a small salon on the ground floor that overlooked the gardens. A maze of hedges disappeared down an incline, the forest I'd seen from my window above invisible from where we were seated.

When I opened my eyes again, the late morning sun had passed over the house, leaving the room in shadow. Minette fluttered nearby, shifting the same ornaments as I came out of my semi-dream state, the ground rocking beneath my feet from some remnant of a dream I couldn't remember.

"You don't have to babysit me," I said tiredly.

When had I become so exhausted? Maybe it was the food. It might have the French touch, but the fare was still heavier than what I was used to. Though, after my stint on the ship, I'd take anything over the hard-tack biscuits with their consistent complement of weevils.

"It's not that, madame," Minette bobbed a quick courtesy. "It's nearly dinner time. The Master will want to eat with you. I think." She slipped the empty glass dangling from my fingers and disappeared into the house's underbelly.

I looked up at Charleton who had appeared at my elbow, keeping a discrete distance between us.

"You should eat with his lordship," he reminded me, gesturing up the hall.

More food? Something groaned within me, but it wasn't my stomach. My feet refused to work, gluing themselves to the worn floorboards beneath my feet.

"I thought he wasn't a lord." My mind returned to the ballroom, the way he'd touched me. Charleton's lips turned up in a kind smile.

"Of course not, madame. He is a viscount, currently, though I believe he left the title when he left his country. But if you find the house...oppressive, my lady, you are welcome at our humble table whenever you wish." He gestured down the hall. A poor cousin to a half-smile returned his sentiment.

"Thank you." I followed him along the corridor.

Minette was already in my room when we arrived

at the door. A heavy brocade draped over her arm, she armed herself with two combs and a bejeweled hair piece.

Charleton left me at my door with assurances my rooms were stocked with all the accompaniments a new wife needed, whatever those might be. "If you are uncertain," his brow furrowed with concern, "yours is the fifth door on the left. The smaller library I mentioned before is across the hall from your room, a door down this way." He gestured to the opposing wall.

I thanked him again; at least I would have something to fill part of my day in the morning. I was halfway down the hall when a thought occurred to me. Pivoting on my heel, I realized he was still waiting at the top of the wide staircase.

He's making sure I don't wander into the wrong room.

"Is there anyone else on this floor?"

Charleton took a step away, casting his face in shadow. There was a pause, and for a moment, I thought he wouldn't answer me.

"His lordship, madame. In the room across from your own."

"Oh."

My mind a blur, I stumbled back to my room to dress for dinner.

Minette primped me in silence while I threw questions in her direction about my husband. Bows tied, curls set, I looked like a show dog, ready to be put through its paces.

"Minette... the portrait gallery." She stared at me,

mute as she'd been the entire night. Had one of the staff told her not to speak to me? The housekeeper, perhaps. I was yet to encounter the formidable personage who must keep command over this tidy household. "When did the family emigrate?"

"Many years ago." Minette disappeared into my hair, tugging curls into a semblance of something fashionable.

"Do you know where they came from?"

Minette hesitated. "Picardie. Fr—"

"France," I finished for her.

Sebastian had come from an area less than half a day's travel from my own. Though mine had disowned me; his, I expected, had not.

"Yes, madame," she whispered, her fingers twitching in my hair.

"*Merci,*" I murmured as she finished her handiwork and collected her things. "The dining hall is...?"

"Down the staircase, along to the left. It opens into a wider room. You won't get lost," she assured me. "Charleton will assist you this evening." A blush rose in her cheeks, combining a pretty mix with her blonde, ringlet hair.

The pink hue suited her. I wondered if I could convince her to wear a hint of it on her half-day off.

I smiled. "And is there a... particular valet who might catch your attention?" A small '*o*' separated her rosebud lips. I hastened to reassure her. "If it is a secret, then I shall keep it for you. I am not someone to be feared."

"No, madame." She bobbed, clutching my trembling hairbrush.

"So, the young man?"

"Oh. Yes, he—that is, James, he—he's been with the house for many years. We grew up together." Eyes round with memory, Minette bobbed again. "Will you need me again tonight, madame?"

"I'm sure he's lovely," I said belatedly. "No. I'll manage to undress myself this evening."

I'd spied the nightdress she'd laid out on the bed, and knew a fresh brick would be waiting at the bottom for me, though the nights were anything but cold.

"He is," she said, smiling brilliantly, returning to our prior conversation. It transformed her from a small, tiny girl, into a radiant young woman.

She left quickly, and I was glad of it—tears sprang to my eyes. While Minette had the memory of her childhood sweetheart, I didn't have a single friend inside the house. I resolved that tomorrow, I would make a few of my own.

Minette did me the favor of laying out attire for dinner after I assured her I would dress myself, unused to being so assisted and waited upon, and having no intent of starting a daily trend now. On special occasions, perhaps. Thankfully, rather than being offended, my new maid selected an ensemble I could get into on my own.

The material was a deep burgundy brocade, heavy, and completely unsuited to the climate here, though that didn't surprise me—women's attire often had little to do with circumstance over what appealed.

As long as we were all kept looking pretty.

Berating myself for my lack of charity in the face of so much—I'd walked off the ship yesterday with naught but a wooden box and the worn dress I arrived in. The more I stared at the brocade that gloved my too-slim figure, the more it reminded me of portraits in houses my father had taken me to visit in years long gone, as a child.

I'd studied those pictures, because none of the men my father befriended seemed to have children, or at least any of my age, and so I was left to wander. The portrait galleries gave me hours of entertainment, and a little fashion-based education. This fabric looked to be two-hundred years or so out of date by continental standards, though by the grace of God—or an amazing seamstress—it was tailored into a newer style.

I gave in to the urge to investigate and flipped the material over. Beneath, new darts and seams had been sewn over older, yellowed threads, bringing the dress into something more of this century. A light over-jacket with a ruffle along the front would hide the altered waistline and changes to the neckline.

Though it didn't need it, I mused; the alterations were masterfully done. I wondered if Minette had a hand in it.

The gown slid on easily enough and wasn't as

heavy as I'd expected, though it did fit like a glove—adding to my suspicion it had been altered for my fit.

I fussed with my hair, straightening loose flowing curls, and added a little powder to my face. It was nothing on what Minette could achieve—I knew her skill in that already—but I'd told the girl she was free for the evening, perhaps to pursue her beau. I wasn't about to break my word so fast and for such a small thing.

If a few loose hairs upset my husband, then we had more problems than what stood at face value. And besides, my resolution was to make friends—and the only people I could do that with was the downstairs staff, if the locale offered nothing else in the realm of population. Besides, I was already in love with their burgeoning relationships. A romantic at heart perchance, but what else should a Parisian be? Maybe that made me a gossip, but a girl had to entertain herself somehow.

A faint rap on my door announced dinner. The sound froze me, my limbs stiff as I stared at the door. The rap came again, and I stepped up to the door and pulled it open, ready to berate the manservant.

"Charleton, I—"

I halted mid-sentence because it wasn't Charleton at all. I stared at an unadorned waistcoat that surrounded a wide chest leading to broad shoulders.

Dressed in a fresh charcoal jacket adorned with colorful embroidery, matched to a black velvet waistcoat and cravat beneath, Sebastian looked impeccable.

My gaze halted at his face. Dark, liquid eyes stared at me from beneath finely-lined brows, giving an appearance of youth, a much older soul lurking beneath his elegant exterior.

The soft black of his cravat provided his alabaster skin with a marbled quality, the deep red of his lips in direct contrast.

For the first time in my life, I felt like a frump.

Even in my singular dress I'd worn from France had I not been so out of place as I was before this man who had taken me to wife.

I am his wife.

While I'd been thinking of him as my husband, I'd forgotten to call myself his wife. Somehow, that elevated status made my observations that much worse. I stilled in my self-consciousness, unwilling to say or do anything that might draw his attention to me but that wasn't by my choice; his gaze lit on me and refused to leave.

I knew the dress I wore was beautiful, but I was insignificant next to the carved beauty before me. Out of my control, my mouth opened but nothing came out. Making sure every muscle did as I asked, I shut it, letting my eyes roam over him.

"I thought we might dine together." He coughed at the false start, proffering his elbow.

"Yes," I nodded. Sliding my fingers around the fine material of his jacket—*is that silk?*—I matched his pace along the hallway, neither of our footsteps making any noise on the heavy carpet. I expected Charleton to be at the top of the stairs where he had been this morning —*was it this morning?*—his absence sitting peculiarly with me. "Charleton mentioned it."

My throat was still dry, regardless of how much I swallowed, so I held my silence for once, praying I wouldn't be like this all night.

"Did he?" The corner of Sebastion's mouth twitched, but I couldn't tell if he was amused or irritated.

Will I ever get to know you?

"Yes," I whispered. My mind blanked, leaving me in that odd void I had experienced in the ballroom with him before.

Sebastian looked down at me, his eyes tinged with amusement, the hidden smile still present at the corners of his mouth. I wondered if he would kiss me, what his mouth pressed over mine would feel like. Lost in his dark gaze, I leaned forward. He paused mid step, pulling me around to his front.

The movement broke my spell, and I gasped, giving my head a small shake to try to clear it. A flush rose in my cheeks, heating my entire face. I was sure I matched the color of my dress.

I'm acting like a virgin on her first outing.

I was, but that was beside the point. I didn't have to act like it.

"Would you like to eat downstairs, or in the library?" His eyes never left mine, but his hand dropped to my waist, slim fingers curving half around it. He seemed so large, his presence so intimidating.

Who the hell had my father sold me to? Who had the *King of France* sold me to?

I smiled, perhaps a little too bright as his eyes narrowed. "The library sounds wonderful." Ahh. My voice returned. That was nice.

"Good," he murmured, turning me in his arms to face a doorway on the opposite side of the hall. His hand shifted to my back as he opened the door, pressing gently.

A shiver rode along my spine at his touch. I was glad of the coat, certain my skin would be covered in *la chair de poule,* should he touch my bare flesh.

I want his touch.

I craved it.

Always so fanciful.

I shook my head and would have bitten back a laugh had that been what tempted my tongue, but it wasn't a laugh that sat behind my closed lips, but a sigh.

Sebastian's firm hand nudged me deeper into the room. I stepped into an intimate library, muffling our steps with carpet as heavy as was fitted out in the rest of the house. A large desk sat at one end of the room. Two winged chairs framed each end of the desk, facing one another across its short length. A bottle of champagne rested between a pair of fine, engraved crystal saucers.

I turned on my heel to face him.

"You knew I would choose the library?" I frowned.

Had he been expecting someone else? My God, did he have a mistress?

Not that a husband taking an extra interest was unusual. France was full of jilted wives and pampered playthings. Even in my innocence I knew of such things. But still...an established mistress provided an ill-fated beginning. Ignoring the spreading jealousy that seeped through my chest—I'd known him for all of a day. No, *known* wasn't the right word. I let my imagination run away for a full second. Then I pulled myself together, looking at my husband for a precious glimpse of clarity.

"I had hoped." That was all he said, guiding me to one of the wingback chairs.

Long, manicured fingers curled around the high back as I seated myself, wishing they were around me, instead.

His proximity alone left my body trembling with overexcited nerves. I took a deep breath, focusing on his slim hand as he poured the effervescent fluid into the glasses where the champagne bubbled and danced within its new confines.

"*Merci*," I murmured, forgetting to speak English for a moment.

"*Je vous en prie.*"

You're welcome.

I started at hearing my native tongue. The words he used were formal, respectful. *He is French.* I knew that, but hearing the words made the familiarity more...real.

True conversation had been lacking in my life since I'd landed in this unknown place.

Sebastian grinned, the simple motion lighting his entire face. It changed him; the formal man fell away, despite his regal way of speaking, blinding me with a look into his real self behind the lord-like facade.

"I forgot you were French." I couldn't escape those eyes, still dark and fathomless, though his smile put me at ease.

"It's good to know I can surprise you." His hand shot out at a blurring speed, cool fingers wrapping around my own in a possessive grip.

My body reacted to his touch in an instant. Heat rushed from my face to settle around my chest, my nipples tightening beneath my coat. I heard my own gasp, jerking in surprise but he held my hand still. The golden liquid in my glass never sloshed, though the flattened goblet sat crooked in my tense grip. Sebastian set my glass upright, not releasing my hand.

"My maid said you have been here for a while?" I stretched for conversation, and this was the best I could come up with? My upbringing failed me daily.

"Did she?" Sebastian lost his smile, repeating the words he'd said earlier in the hall. His thumb brushed over the inside of my wrist, resting against my pulse. "What else did your maid say?" His gaze sharpened, narrowing on me.

A thrill tore down my spine, my breath hitching until he lowered his gaze, and I could breathe again. I made a note to never let him know something one of the staff said to me, or that I had designs to befriend them. Such prejudices weren't unusual in our culture, similar to a man taking a mistress despite a willing wife at his side or in his bed.

Bias was more than common within the nobility, as much as it was within the lower classes, though their outlook was more deserved, in my view.

I tugged my wrist free as my past and present collided in a mix of memories that threw my focus away for a moment. Months in a single dress on a ship when my father had essentially sold me as the King's whore would do that. After all, a woman paid for sex was still a courtesan and was simply a bird of an unusual color in my rank.

That thought had run about my head the entire trip, though I had never acknowledged it until now. Was that how Sebastian saw me? A paid, painted woman?

"Afraid the archangel will take you, courtesan?"

The nun's words as the unnamed abbey filtered through my mangled thoughts. Swallowing my fear, I refocused on the man before me. *My husband.*

His family must have been affluent for many years —though considering my dress, I wondered if he had fallen on hard times out in the wilds of the new world, or if he struggled with the different cultures the Americas presented.

"Do you not vet your own staff?" I asked, then shook my head, softening my tone. "Min—She has been very welcoming, very helpful." I clamped my mouth shut over my waffling before I mentioned the events in the *other* library.

Sebastian held my gaze a moment longer then nodded, seemingly to himself. He uncovered a plate of *amuse-bouche*; a term whose literal translation meant *bites of food to amuse the mouth*. Back home, they were considered a delicacy, presented at a chef's whim. Sebastian must be on very good terms with his.

He slid the plate my way. I took a bite, delicate, flaky pastry dissolving into a savory center. Flavor filled my mouth, the sensation so good, so like home at my father's table when my mother still lived, that I could have moaned.

Dark eyes pinned me in place. His study tore away all the barriers I'd put in place, curling my hair, dressing in finery that felt both like him and a false-hood all at once. Determined not to falter before him, I peered around the small library.

Wood paneled walls were covered with floor-to-ceiling rows of books. Most looked quite old, and I couldn't wait to learn what my husband stocked in his private library, because surely this space was his own workplace. Why else keep such a diminutive room, when there were so many others, larger and better suited to the purpose in his home?

A small cough brought me back to the meal. "You're not eating."

A home where servants cut themselves in a bid to escape this place.

The drawn curtains suggested a monster hidden in

plain sight, a face amongst the masses of servants hired with the sole purpose of serving a single master...and now me.

I quashed the foreboding in my stomach, hoping it wasn't the food—which was amazing. *Mon Dieu,* could the fare be poisoned? As though reading my mind, Sebastian huffed. The corners of his mouth turned up again—definitely a smile this time.

Unsure whether to fake an emotion I didn't feel or run screaming from the room and let my fancies get the better of my senses, I placed my fork beside the half-empty plate with deliberate gentleness.

When did I become a glutton?

"Is this a joke to you? Am *I*?" I couldn't finish the sentence and regretted saying anything.

What if he answered me, confirming my suspicions? Would I hide in my room for the rest of my life? Run away?

And been eaten by alligators? Don't be daft.

For once, I agreed with the little voice in my head.

Sebastian rose from the other end of the short desk. His height—enough that I needed to tilt my head back to catch his gaze if I were standing next to him—filled the room, constricting the air to a choking point.

When he leaned forward, halting over me, a predatory expression crossed his face, a feral thing both ancient and inviting. My back arched in response to his pose, my head tilted back. His smirk promised sin, and darker things.

I might be safer with the alligators.

CHAPTER SIX

GISELLA

I couldn't tear my gaze away from Sebastian as he stalked the few paces toward me. For a single moment, he towered over me, then dropped to his heels, kneeling on the floor at my side.

A wash of coolness swept over me, like he was both there and not, all at once. He studied me; dark eyes boring into my own, reaching to the corners of my soul. But it wasn't the clinical probing a local *docteur* might inflict, rather that coolness turned to a comforting warmth, spreading through me as the world narrowed down to him alone.

One hand rose, his fingers curling inches from my skin before he dropped them, the moment broken by his jarring movement. The ghost of his touch caressed my cheek where his phantom touch had been a second ago. A swipe of his deft fingers flicked away the short jacket I wore, exposing my shoulders. The material slithered off my arms. I clutched it to my stomach as a pithy shield.

His mouth turned up in a rueful smile. "I've taken liberties with you, haven't I? After all, you've just arrived. I forget things like...time."

Though he stared into my eyes—right through me —Sebastian seemed far distant from where we sat, lost somewhere in a place I couldn't reach. He blinked, as though rushing back to our shared present. Where he had gone in that moment?

He was right; I knew little about him, and he knew as much about me, though I suspected he might have collected more information about who I was on the journey from the abbey to our home. His home. Was it mine now, too? Not in the monetary sense, but would I call this place home forever now?

I had spent so many months in transit, uncertain. A guest in abbey after abbey, with no place to find solidarity in my fate. Now I had that, it seemed more tenuous than ever.

His soft laugh brought me back. "I'm not the only one with an odd sense of time." He offered a small smile to ease his words, turning them from an insult to a...something else. An offering, perhaps.

That tiny bridge brought me a little closer to him. When he spoke, I detected the very faint undercurrent of an accent lilting his words. If I hadn't been from France, from his province, I doubted I would have noticed it at all.

"I arrived..." I trailed off, trying to think when it had been, and realized that in the rush of everything that had happened, I had no idea what the date was— or when we had landed in New Orleans. I offered a wan smile. "Perhaps I'm more tired than I thought."

A pathetic offering, and by Sebastian's creased brow, he agreed.

"I've been a poor host."

"Husband."

"I beg your pardon?"

"You're my husband. Not...not a poor husband. Just that you are one. Mine," I ended feebly, wishing I'd never opened my mouth at all.

His mouth pressed into a line. Neither thick nor thin—his arched lips a rosy hue, not the over plumpness of the courtiers of home, too soft, too indulged, though I knew his smile could curl something in my chest alongside his lips.

"Yes," he replied, canting his head, as though thinking it over. "I am your husband, aren't I?"

His eyes caught mine again, drifting downwards, over my decolletage, to the concave curve of a traveler's stomach. When his hooded gaze rose to meet mine, dark desire lingered there.

My cheeks heated, knowing what must come.

Do you want this or don't you, Gisella?

A voice echoed in my head, and with a start, I thought it was his. *It's not my choice.* I became his property the moment I married...him. My cheeks burned. If I couldn't concentrate on this moment, he would write me off as a simpleton, and I'd be left to myself for who knew how long.

I'd heard of arranged marriages where the partners lived their own lives, took on a group of friends in a lonely life, but here? Here, there was no one but me, Sebastian, and the servants. I shook myself, trying to get my head straight, and took a sip of champagne.

Bubbles fizzed about my lips, sending the alcohol to my head.

"You are," I said softly, unsure what question I answered, clutching my napkin as he returned to his assessment.

"Then there are some things we need to talk about." Sebastian straightened his legs with a long sigh, as though he were an old man and the weight of the world rested upon him.

"What—um, things?" I twiddled my napkin until it frayed at one end, sipping my champagne with my other hand.

The flush went straight down, this time, heating my chest. My nipples tightened, their hard outline visible at the edge of the fabric constraining my dress, though I daren't look down to see what color my pale skin turned. I sighed, slipping my coat back a little to ease the warmth that left me languid beneath his gaze.

"Gisella—" My husband straightened, and I realized how close he sat.

"Seb—"

Our names collided. He planted his fists on the back of my chair, looming over me. When had he moved closer? My breath shortened, and I was sure I'd pop a button or something.

He leaned closer, his breath kissing my lips when he paused. A visible shudder wracked him, his grip on the chair back stretching the fabric behind my shoulders.

"I should—Gella—" He used the name I'd preferred since childhood without knowing, and I accepted it, without thought.

"You should," I whispered, and wrapped my hands around his collar, tugging him down to me.

His lips found mine, pressing hard at first, then softening, exploring. His tongue swept across the seam of my lips, and I gasped at the intimate caress. The tension that wound tight inside me all day unspool as he thrust his tongue roughly inside my mouth, then as his kisses before danced in light flicks against my own.

I followed his movements as though it were a waltz for two alone, letting him lead and learning how he wanted me to respond to his silent commands. My body fizzed with need and aches I'd never experienced in my life. Flirtations in Paris were so commonplace that they meant little to nothing at all.

This experience was well outside my own frame of reference. Every touch, every kiss left me craving more of him. Cool fingers brushed my warmed cheek, knuckles grazing my jawline as he tipped my head back, slanting his mouth across mine until he arced over my body. I moved with him, seeking more contact, more kisses...*more*.

His hands tangled in my hair, fisting the loose ends as he deepened the kiss. A moan slipped from my lips, or maybe it was his. It didn't matter; we were both as lost in each other, our bodies entangled and fighting against clothing that got in the way of our discovery. One arm slipped behind my waist, lifting me against his hard form to pull me closer.

The fabric of my jacket curled back as though by his will alone. It dropped to the floor, leaving my shoulders bare to his hungry touch. When his cool hands pressed flush to my back, I whimpered. He traced my shoulder blades, long fingers sliding beneath my dress as I clung to him, swept away in the emotion.

Sensation whirled around me in a dizzying montage of hands and lips and tongues. My skin heated wherever he touched me, his hands tugging at the edge of my dress.

"Wait," I gasped, breathless, as the eyelets holding the material together began to part. I clutched my dress up, pressing it to my chest. "Sebastian, shouldn't we...?"

Be in a bed? Wasn't that the proprietary thing to do? His touch, so experienced over my innocence, reminded me how little I knew of what a marriage was supposed to be beyond Amy's strange interludes and stories I weren't sure whether to believe in, or not.

His soft laugh brushed the edges of my mind, his kisses trailing along my throat to the curve of my ear. Without offering me an answer Sebastian sucked and licked at the sensitive spot there until I cried out; a wanton sound that left me in a realm of embarrassment and pure need. Heat gushed between my legs, a sweet ache tingling swollen flesh there.

"We should," he said firmly.

The material at my breast tugged tight. An eyelet popped free, then another. Pulling me from the chair Sebastian braced me against, he dragged us to the floor, kneeling over me. Strong arms cradled my weight until my head met the plush carpet with a gentle bump, then his mouth was on mine again, and I couldn't think at all.

Swaths of material tangled around my legs. I twisted, flicking at the knotted fabric until I could move again. Sebastian grasped my waist, his hands encompassed me, and jerked my body up to meet his. That arched, wicked mouth still punishing mine, he pulled me hard against his chest.

My world inverted, blood rushing in both directions. Every kiss left me senseless and overwhelmed, reacting to his touch by pure instinct. I explored his shoulders and chest, running over the planes of muscle there, the curves and ridges beneath his fine shirt.

He groaned, shucking the offending article over his head. Red lips parted, he stared down at me like I was the last meal he'd ever eat and was determined to gorge himself. His chest heaved, a slick of sweat gracing his hard muscle, giving him a carved quality. As though he wasn't quite of this time, or any other.

Sucking in a long, shuddering breath of my own, needing the calming, cool air to soothe the heat that flushed me head to toe, I reached tentative, trembling hands to run my fingertips over the lines of his stomach.

Sebastian stopped breathing altogether, his jaw clenched, eyes wreathed in dark flame that went on and on behind a dark soul lingering there. His silence offered a sort of permission. I resumed my journey, running over hard ridges of lean muscle, tracing the tight peaks of his chest.

The breath he held hissed between his teeth, but he didn't stop me from touching him. Braced on one forearm, his grip around my waist loosened, sliding along my backbone. Spikes of painful pleasure followed his caress. I arched with the sensation, surrendering my body to his touch. He tugged my corset down, the tips of my breasts springing free above my chemise that he shredded seconds later.

Groaning, he dipped his head to suck my nipple into his mouth, returning his hand to my hair with his other, pulling my head back. My throat bared to him, he pulled my body into an arch, and held me there. Lips and tongue teased my nipple, tugging and nipping. A sharp sting left me crying out. His gaze raised to meet mine.

The predator in him stared out at me, undisguised. I cried out again as he shifted his hold to capture both my wrists, pinning them at my back.

"Do not fight me." The command in his voice was evident.

I nodded, unable to draw in a full breath to answer him.

Something in his eyes flickered as I submitted to his will, giving my body over to his demands. His fingers still tangled in my long hair, I remained in my arch, captive to his needs.

His smile grew as he watched my struggle. The points of my nipples ached. I tilted my shoulders back, shameless in my desire for his mouth on my skin. His breath brushed the breast he tortured, a single flick of his tongue drawing a long sound from my throat.

I strained at his hold, needing to touch him, to drag his mouth to my breast and encourage him to suck, but I had no leverage or strength against his impenetrable grip. His control absolute, I could do nothing but submit to his hold over my body and let him do as he pleased.

And I wanted to submit to him.

Laughing softly at my predicament, Sebastian shifted to feast on my other breast. His kisses and nips left me drowning in a sea of pleasure and pain. I arched deeper against him, aligning my half-exposed body to his, needing the contact. Pleasure built between my thighs, slicing new pathways inside my body to where he sucked on my nipples, alternating and teasing until I crested the wave, my body liquid and easy against his harder form.

A sharp pain hit me, knocking me further into

oblivion. Reality spun away from me, coiled in a ribbon of pleasure that went on and on. Sebastian's voice whispered half-words in my mind, as though he commanded that, too. I swam closer to those sounds, but they shut off as fast, a dreamlike realm where nothing was ever truly attainable.

His hand in my hair tugged me back to reality. I tangled bare legs around his thighs, the hardness of him rigid and urgent against my heat. I didn't remember removing our clothes, but let him take charge, unable—unwilling—to fight him for dominance. I craved his touch, ached for him between my thighs. He nudged my body, slicking us both in my desire.

"Wider," he murmured, pausing until I did as he asked.

I sighed my pleasure over and over, sinking deeper against the floor, my hands open at my sides.

"Gella," he whispered, his voice straining.

I moaned against his shoulder, shifting against his body. *Don't stop. Please, never, ever stop.* "What are you—"

I blinked at the man, the *monster* before me. His mouth glistened red, twin scarlet trails framing his perfect mouth. The logical part of my brain noted the discrepancy in a dispassionate way, as though I weren't the reason his mouth was coated with my blood. I made the mistake of looking down at my breast.

Two small puncture marks indented the skin against the dusky pink of my nipple. A thin stream trickled over the swell of my breast. I watched as Sebastian lowered his mouth to my pale skin and lapped at the blood, smearing the scarlet trail across his mouth and me.

Torn between the awareness of my nakedness and the need to cover myself, my mind chose to focus on a growing horror, the understanding in my mind of who —*what*—my husband was. I wriggled beneath his weight, frantic to move away, to be *anywhere else* but near him, beneath him.

Don't. Move.

A whisper in my mind reminded me of the bliss he offered as he sucked at my breast in a twisted parody of mother and child, life giving sustenance. Heat bloomed anew in my belly.

His tongue worked my nipple, pulling and tugging once again until he broke free of my skin with a loud *pop*. A scream built in my throat as he watched me, too calm, knowing he maintained ultimate control of the situation while I writhed beneath him, helpless.

Prey.

Between my legs, a finger delved into my wet heat and flicked once. I gasped, still pulling away, though my hands tangled themselves around his arms, pulling and pushing away at the same time. The finger flicked a second time, tracing the outline of my nether lips, learning the shape of me.

My cheeks burned as my own desire reflected in his eyes. Then my gaze dropped to his lips, red still staining the skin there. I pressed back into the thick carpet, my hips rising of their own volition to meet his touch.

Desperate to get away from him while my flesh demanded I drew nearer, I gasped again, moaning as his finger slid to the knuckle inside me. Sebastian held me tight, bands of iron arms surrounding my back, preventing me from moving away.

"Please—I have to—" I tore at his arms, my eyes latched to his, as his tongue cleaned the red from his teeth and lips.

My blood.

Rocking my hips against his hand, I watched in fascinated silence, unable to tear my gaze away from the horror caressing my body in such an intimate way.

"Gella," he said again, his voice thick and rough, reaching around me, pulling me closer as his touch paused, though his finger still filled me. "Don't fight me, little hellion of a wife."

Ruby lips hovered over mine, the tip of his tongue flickering out to taste my mouth. I pulled back, but the action was half-hearted, and we both knew it. Heat gushed between my legs, coating his hand in a way I couldn't hide my reaction to his monster, his authority. Something—*triumph, victory?*—lit his eyes as he dipped his mouth down to mine.

The same lips that dripped with my blood.

His mouth crashed against mine, his other hand sliding down my back, to press me against him, harder onto the demands he made of my body. Fear abandoned sense, giving way to the infatuating need to be closer, melding our bodies together.

I cupped my hands to his cheeks, opening my lips to his kiss as his fingers and tongue dueled for dominance within me. Over me.

Mine.

His voice caressed my mind, and I jerked back, staring. A shadow of implicit knowledge flickered in his face. His eyes held mine, a challenge to defy him written there.

I didn't.

He slammed his hands into the carpet beside my head, his breath cool against my searing pulse. I rolled to one side, folding my arms around my body. My mind still revolted at the idea of the man I had married while my body craved him like an opium eater deep in his den.

Sebastian grabbed my hands, pressing my wrists to my sides, apart from my body. Holding me in place he knelt back, watching. *Longing.* My nails imprinted on my palms, the biting pain dousing the edge of my arousal the slightest amount.

His much larger hands pressed over mine, entwining our hands in a hard squeeze. "Don't hurt yourself," he murmured, uncurling my fingers in one hand and kissing each one, and then doing the same to the other hand before he pinned my wrists where they had been. This time, I let him. "Gella, you're beautiful. So, so beautiful." His body settled over mine, every inch of him finding a place against me.

If I hurt you, I beg my forgiveness with pleasure.

His mouth descended on mine as he worked his way between my hips and thrust forward.

Stars exploded behind my eyes. Not the pleasurable sort, but a deep tear that centered around where he pushed his length inside me. I whimpered against his perfect, arched lips.

His tongue speared inside my mouth, and I tasted my own blood. "I promised you pleasure with pain, Gella," he murmured.

The ache remained as he thrust all the way inside me. His breath left mine and I inhaled until sharp points pierced my throat, and my world exploded again. Pure bliss filled my body, overwhelmed my mind. My hips undulated as he began to move within me, smooth, slow strokes that matched the gentle rhythmic suck at my pulse.

I arched and curled around him, as he released me, trailing my hands over his back, his shoulders. His hips moved against mine, smooth movements turning rough. Teeth grazed my throat, sharp strings against my skin over and over again until I gushed hot and liquid in his arms. I cried out, tangling my hands in his hair.

Somewhere in the depths of my mind, he growled a low possessive sound.

You'll always be mine, Gella.

CHAPTER SEVEN

GISELLA

I lay on my stomach in the cool air, Sebastian's body warm where our flesh touched, as though by being near the living, it gave him life. He tangled his hands in my hair, alternating gentle strokes and tugs, a sweet mirror of the way he played with my breasts, of his hips pummeling relentlessly into me.

A gentle ache between my legs reminded me of the way his body owned mine, a dampness there that belonged to both of us.

I raised myself on my elbows over his chest, looking down at him. "Is this what you had in mind, tonight?" Though my awkwardness had dropped away, I was unsure what to say and sought to fill the silence, anyway.

"Well, I did have something in mind," he

murmured, capturing my face in both hands and pressing a kiss to my mouth with blood-stained lips. "For now, be still, you little hellion, and let me worship you." His eyes laughed at me while my mind stumbled over my acceptance of who and *what* I had married.

But accepted him, I had.

I shook my head in mock horror. "Defiling virgins in their new home..."

"Did I hurt you?" he asked seriously, drawing me down to him. His mouth found mine, gentle, undemanding, this time.

If I hurt you, I beg forgiveness with pleasure.

My body heated at the memory of his prowess in the sexual arts. Could a woman want less in an arranged proposal? I shook my head, bemused. The brief pain where he'd bitten me revisited me in a sharp pang. But that wasn't what he'd meant, and anyway, I wasn't prepared to have that conversation quite yet.

As though he were present in my head, his hand came down on the soft flesh of my rump, the memory of pain and pleasure reviving my desire. I yelped, and he did it again, smiling as I writhed on his lap. Each smack built pressure inside my body, and as promised, he paired the pleasure of a sweet stroke along my soaked folds between blows.

I trembled, clinging to him as he worked out whatever he needed as he probed my deeper places with a single finger. Each stroke of pain or pleasure brought another moan from my lips. He studied me as I writhed on his prostrate body as though cataloging my cries and storing them away for later, when he might make me scream for him again.

After an interminable time, he offered quarter, working his fingers in quick, hard strokes deep inside me. My cries grew as I stared down into his face, letting him command my body until I broke, shattering over him and slumped onto his chest. My pants softened as he cupped the back of my head and held me to him, my legs slipped either side of his wide body.

I didn't know how long we lay together, tangled in each other's arms. As my awareness came back, so did my prior thoughts. I leaned up to lick his chest, earning a soft groan.

"Gella, if you do things like that—" His warning sent a frisson of heat through my exhausted body.

Not to be deterred, I asked the question that was most on my mind.

"It was you, with the maid. Wasn't it?" She hadn't hurt herself after all. He had. I didn't need to ask, but saying the words aloud made the surreal circumstances seem so much more ...real, somehow. "I should be scared of you," I mused, burying my head against his chest.

I'd searched for a heartbeat before, and found none.

At least the legend didn't disappoint.

"Not everyone is so...*accepting* of my kind." The lamp flickered, throwing his face into sharp relief, enhancing the angle of his jaw, the high cheekbones and shadows around his eyes.

"That's understandable," I murmured, burrowing closer, despite the implied horror of his words. "People fear what they don't know."

"And you know me now, do you?" His voice took on a hint of amusement, fast swallowed by a harsh laugh. "I was created by a creature who dined on magic and slept on a bed of souls. She—" His face shuttered, the demonic look leaving him until he appeared human again, except for the tinge of blood that stained his lips. "I don't know if there are more like me. Who, or *what* she might have made. I was purely an experiment. If I have kin, she forgot to mention it as she terrorized life from a broken body."

Light fingertips trailed my cheek. He wound my hair around his fingers, tugging insistently. I raised my head, sucking in a long breath.

Why aren't I afraid of you?

Fathomless eyes fixed on mine, amusement roiling in their shadowy depths. Hurt and something deeper lay beneath the facade, the cover he must use with everyone else.

There are no others, Gella. It is just us, and my staff.

I blinked, listening to his voice within my mind. His presence rested there, amongst the unseen places in my head. Not at all intrusive, more company I hadn't known I was lacking.

Have you always been there?

But there was no answer, so I asked him again, the

usual way. So fast my perceptions had changed. I frowned, knowing I should have more questions, be less accepting of his...situation. As though something was wrong inside me.

Yes. Since you came to New Orleans.

I started, pulling away, but his long arms coiled around me, trapping in his embrace against his chest. I let him press me against his skin, what I'd wanted from the outset of our encounter. Before he taught me so many things about both my body and his.

Before he withdrew from my body, rubbed his fingers in the mixed fluids coating his cock and licked my virgin blood from his fingers.

My concept of what comprised a villain reset every time I learned something new about him.

"You should be afraid of me." His chest rumbled beneath my cheek while he resumed threading through my hair. "Why aren't you afraid? Of me," he added as an afterthought.

I smiled, listening to the nothingness where his heart should beat. "I had... a moment," I confessed, mimicking the patterns he made in my hair on his chest with my fingertips. A shudder ran over him, small bumps rising on his skin. *Something of life remains within him.* A different sort of life, perhaps. I smiled at the thought that I could get a reaction from him. "When I saw the blood—my blood..." I trailed off, the image of his lips glistening red.

But no force of repulsion followed that thought, no fear.

"A *moment*?" Amusement laced his tone—true amusement, this time.

I propped myself back on my elbows, looking down at him.

Ebony arched eyebrows curved against marble, smooth, and perfectly angled. *Soft, over the hardness within.*

"Gella," he murmured. His fingers tangled deeper into my hair, and I thought he would pull me down to him. "Why aren't you afraid?"

"I—" I waited for my head to come up with some logical reason. But the organ I relied on in my lifetime failed me. *Thank you for the warning.* I whispered the note to myself. "I have no idea."

"You should be." His brow furrowed, eyes narrowing as he studied me.

I shrugged, uncomfortable beneath his assessing gaze. "Well, I'm not. So…"

"So." His eyes cleared. "It appears I have a wife."

Some emotion swelled in me at his words. I tried to swallow past the lump in my throat, which warred with the nest of worms roiling in my belly. Why I should care so much for an ideal I hadn't put stock in from the moment my father sold me and left me in a nunnery? Certainly not with a man I'd met but had been promised to at some previous, unknown date, I couldn't say.

Sebastian crushed me against his chest, cradling me tight to his body as though he never wanted to let me go.

Domineering, controlling...monster. I knew what he was; what the girls on the ship and I had contrived to have the other passengers believe, who shied away from us, fear and repulsion in their eyes. Now, I was in the arms of one such creature, and all I felt was...relief. *Trust.* A long breath left me. I relaxed into his hold and closed my eyes.

A sharp knock on the library door roused me; I glanced down to find Sebastian sleeping deeply. With no breath escaping his lips, he looked...different. I frowned, ignoring the repeated knocking, pressing my hand to his cheek. His flesh was cold as it had been before, but harder, somehow. As though life had left him.

The door creaked open behind me. I shrieked, rolling off Sebastian's still form, scrambling at my sides in a frantic effort for cover, huddling in the remnants of my dress.

"Charleton!"

"Oh, my— Madame, I am so sorry—"

The butler, I really *did* need to learn his title, hovered at the door frame, his sharp gaze taking in his disrobed master, me by his side, my throat covered in flaking blood. Despite his flustered apology, some part of my mind noted that he hadn't retreated from the room, either.

What a sight—though I doubted it was the first time he had come across such a scene. Somewhere in my chest, a tiny monster roared with jealousy at the image of another woman in my husband's arms. *At least he's not the single monster here,* I thought wryly.

I managed to gather the tatters of my dress around me, but my husband had efficiently ripped the whole thing down the middle—no wonder it had come off so easily. Keeping it around my shoulders was nigh impossible, and as Charleton had probably seen more of my naked hide than he'd ever expected, it was a moot point. The Lord above knew what my hair looked like.

Settling for gripping the material to my side and leaving my shoulders bare, I straightened, attempting the pretense of some sort of lady-like posture. Charleton's face went bright red as he surveyed me, half draped over his employer. His face reflected my suspicions of my hair, but I decided to keep up the pretense anyway.

"What did you need, Charleton?"

The valet's lips twitched as his color began to return to some semblance of normal—*what was considered normal, in this place?*—and opened his mouth.

I had no idea what he expected to come out, but the tall, thin man snorted a laugh.

A giggle escaped my lips. I clapped a hand over my mouth, clutching the material tight beneath my armpit, but I couldn't stop. Both of us doubled with laughter, Charleton clinging to the doorway, me over my husband's prone body.

Inappropriate, Gella.

I gasped as Sebastian berated me in my head.

Charleton stopped laughing, peering around fearfully, his shoulders raised to his ears.

"Did—do you hear him, too?" I whispered, the breath of Sebastian's apparent powers astounding me.

Charleton nodded, his lips pressed in a thin line, unspeaking.

I took a deep breath.

"Wake up." I leaned over Sebastian's still form, but he remained unresponsive. I tapped his face. Not so much as a flicker of his eyelids. Contemplating slapping him harder to see if I could get a reaction, I expected him to open his eyes, scare me as a child does, pretending a hurt.

Hands settled on my—very bare—shoulders, and I jumped a mile.

"*Jesu Christus*, Charleton," I swore, looking over my shoulder, crossing myself by habit.

The corners of his mouth turned down. "He won't wake," he said softly.

Something inside my head agreed, but I pushed on, my logical brain aware and rearing, finally. "What do you mean, he *won't wake*? He was fine and, um, active an hour ago."

It was my turn to flush, heat rising from the line of material to above my eyebrows. I wouldn't have been surprised had steam issues from the top of my head.

"But, madame. The sun is rising. He does not...exist...in the moment of light as it breaks on God's day."

Well put.

"It's morning?" I glanced at the hall behind him,

then realized the fruitlessness of the action. "You don't need to be scared of him, Charleton," I said, searching for a way to lift the body beneath me.

Sebastian exhibited no sign of life bar the frustrating commentary running through my head. I glanced at Charleton, still checking the room around us.

Actually, he does.

Charleton jumped and scurried from the room.

"Would you stop doing that?" I asked in exasperation, addressing Sebastian's corpse in front of me. Nothing odd about that, talking to a lifeless body bearing my husband's likeness beneath me. "You've scared the man half to death."

Why aren't you afraid, Gella?

"He works for you," I reminded him, wondering how on earth we were going to move him. Sebastian seemed to have gained hundreds of pounds in his sleep. Death? Charleton's words came back to me, and doubt began to grow deep inside me.

"Can you blame me?" I snapped, continuing my soliloquy and attempting to tug his shirt over his chest. His broad, well-defined chest. My hands passed over ridges of muscle. I swallowed, tracing outlines of his physique.

Are you quite done?

Desisting in groping the man, I returned to tugging the material over him, and moved to his pants, struggling to get them around his round, firm buttocks.

You've never dressed a man, have you?

"I'm so glad you find this amusing." My irritation growing, I sat back. *Defeated by men's breeches.* "How do you dress with all this?" Flustered, I gestured to his half-covered form as though he could see me.

You should talk. That dress took far too long to remove.

"Mhmm." I didn't dignify that with a proper reply. "Is Charleton likely to be back?"

Perhaps. He's seen me in worse states.

"This happens often, does it?" I imagined a string of women scooting from his bedroom, terrified and under threat of silence. "Wait, what do you mean, *worse states*?"

That's a discussion for when I can speak to you properly.

"What, this isn't *properly*?" I grumbled, expecting a snarky reply, but there was none. "Sebastian?"

The room grew cold, as though his presence had left, though his body remained. Tugging my clothes around me, I surveyed his still form as I rose.

Where do you go?

Silence met my thoughts.

No matter how many times I called out to him, Sebastian either didn't hear me or refused to respond. Giving it up as a bad job and assuming someone with greater strength than me or the man himself would do something about his exposed body, I towed my worn, exhausted body to the door. I peeked around the hallway, but Charleton and his flock of staff who scampered everywhere together had disappeared.

I crossed the corridor to my own room, closing the

door behind me. A shiver took over my body, most likely from a combination of blood loss, exhaustion and the trauma of being a nail bed for my husband's teeth. With that bitter thought in mind, I dropped the tattered material of my ruined dress to the floor.

Not bothering to dress or bathe, I collapsed into the comfort of the bed and fell asleep.

CHAPTER EIGHT

GISELLA

I rolled in the bed, the brick at my feet a comfort against the cool body beside me. Memory of hands and lips and tongue blissed me out for a long enough moment for my body to relax against his harder form at my back.

I smiled in my dozy state—Minette must have heated the brick and pulled the blankets around me—at last thought, I'd toppled on top of the lot, and lay still in my bed as frozen as Sebastian when she came in to check on me.

I slept away the day until sun turned to moon. Then, Sebastian found me, his lips pressed to my throat, sucking in sweet, gentle kisses to reopen the wounds there as his fingers played between my legs, and I opened my body and mind to him, wanton for the all-encompassing pleasure that besieged me.

My cries could have raised the dead, or maybe the household, but he didn't seem to care. When he was done drinking, his hand curled around my throat, holding me pinned in place while his mouth devoured mine and his fingers teased me until I sank against his body, exhausted yet again.

The last thing I remembered before I succumbed back to the dream realm, was his laughter filled apology for waking me, that he fed and I hadn't.

His arms left me safe and protected, and I didn't care enough for food to break away from him in my dozed state, my body humming with his touch as he eased me into his arms.

Despite his apology, some part of my mind noted that he hadn't retreated from the room, either.

Sebastian.

His hand slid along my legs, dipping into the curve of my waist. I already knew his touch, the length and pressure of his fingers familiar. Palming my stomach, he pulled me back against him. I forced my eyes open to see the night sky outside the window—though it wasn't mine. No small balconette, no arch. This window was square and took up most of the wall space.

I sat, the blankets puddling around my waist. The wandering hand paused on my hip.

"We're in your room?" I guessed, not turning around.

Waves drew along the coastline below the house. I'd thought he lived inland, but somehow my senses had been turned around during my wine-filled, night time journey. His room must face the back of the house, away from the gardens and forest I could view from mine.

From the mansion's second story, I couldn't see where the sludge and forests turned to tepid waters no doubt infected with the same prehistoric reptilian monsters.

His hands slipped around my waist, pulling me around, back to him, and I was met with those eyes that pierced my entire being. A shiver passed over me. I wasn't the only one unclothed.

Swallowing hard, I twisted to look over my shoulder, clutching the sheet at my waist, hair tumbling haphazardly around my bare shoulders.

Heat burned within Sebastian's gaze. His eyes never left my face, though I had the impression he took in all of me where I sat. He crooked a finger—the small movement sending a thrill through me as he drew me up his chest.

"Uh-uh," I wriggled. "You promised to talk."

Sebastian's features smoothed. "Always with the talking."

Two days of sex, of learning about the monster in my bed, let alone under it, swirled around me in a maelstrom of emotion. I couldn't pick one down to focus on, and suddenly, everything was too much.

"Answer me," I whispered.

Tears stung my eyes when he stared at me, stone faced. *Don't do this to me.* I pleaded inside my head, hoping our silent conversation hadn't been a figment of my imagination. The dual ache at my throat and breast certainly wasn't.

I slapped his chest, but he didn't move. No mark rose beneath his skin, though my hand stung.

"So you are—" I faltered, still staring.

"I am."

I slapped him again, though it appeared to make no difference to him. "Don't you do that."

"Do what?" His face was smooth as alabaster, though I sensed a large degree of humor boiling beneath the surface.

"That," I snapped, though the single word came out waspish. I swallowed and tried again. "Don't you go all god-like on me."

His hands clamped around my hips, and he rolled me beneath him with ease.

Maybe chastising a minor god wasn't the best idea of the morning. Or night. My mind flitted back to the first day here— yesterday, today...my thoughts remained too muddled, my sense of time lost.

I'd thought my husband was a lay-about who chose to rise in the evenings on my first day. Not that those hours were that different from the rest of European nobility, but the truth had been far more haunting.

Sebastian snarled above me, his weight bearing down on the body he had spent so many hours teasing and using for his own pleasure while giving me mine

Definitely god-like.

"Do I look god-like to you?" he growled, the sound reverberating through his broad chest.

Without much thought in the action and lost in the feel of him, I nodded. His snarl grew as he pushed my thighs apart, sinking his hard length inside me in a single stroke.

I tossed my head back, my mouth dry on the scream that tore from my throat.

Then his lips were there, sucking as he worked his hips into me over and over, his hands gripping my rear for purchase. I swallowed the wave of pleasure threatened to black out the twin pain and pleasure as he rose to kiss me. Ruby lips glinted in the darkness, my body responding to his every wish.

Then he kissed me, demanding more, and then the night swallowed us both.

His fingers trailed the length of my spine as I rested on his chest, my body covered with a fine sheen of sweat. Sebastian's, of course, held nothing. I sighed, tracing a hand over the ridges of muscle on his chest, down to his stomach.

"You're too perfect." I propped my elbows on his chest, remembering the last time I'd done this, and hoped we wouldn't be interrupted.

"You think I'm perfect?" His mouth twisted in a sardonic smile. "You don't know anything about me,

Gella." His voice was as dark as his eyes, like velvet that wrapped around me.

An edge of danger tugged at me, heightening all my senses.

I thought about what I did know—which wasn't that much—of his resilience to the bias against his kind, and there was plenty I needed to discuss with him. There was the way the servants were around him —had he terrified them for years? And the Gallery. That strong familial resemblance I suspected was the singular lifetime of one man.

Yet another conversation I needed to have. But he hadn't killed me, hadn't maimed me, though he contained the strength and ability to do so.

A wife would be easy to replace in such a remote home.

I winced at the thought—mine, not his—and prayed I hadn't gotten it wrong. It didn't matter much if I had; there was nowhere to flee to, nowhere to run.

I doubted I could outrun the beast of the man who hid behind the arrogant, crafted exterior of a much older lord, and shivered. The frisson of fear followed a hot dose of arousal that painted my thighs with slick need. I stared at his mouth, wondering if he would kiss me again, my lips still swollen and tender from our lovemaking.

My brain drew itself away from tracing his amazing physique with my eyes to ask a question—one of far too many cluttered in there. I started with the hardest one I brought up before, but he hadn't answered me, not really. Sebastian was a master of evasion.

"The maid—I thought she'd harmed herself. But she hadn't, had she? Charleton covered for you."

His mouth set in a hard line. For a moment, I thought he wouldn't answer me again, then he let out a soft sigh.

"Yes." His gaze held mine, steady. "I'm the monster you need worry about here."

"I'm grateful it was her neck, not her breast, married man," I murmured. "Or you'd be in trouble."

He spluttered laughter, sitting up while he choked. I thumped his back unhelpfully.

"Oh, Gella," He wiped tears from his eyes, and gathered me in his arms. I slipped my legs around his waist, pressing close. "You are certainly unique."

You can call me crazy. There's nowhere for me to hide, anyway.

I let the thought linger between us, then revolved back to my line of questions. "Do you force them to be here? The servants," I clarified.

"Things are not done here as they are in France." He stroked my hair, pulling the covers around me, though it wasn't a cold morning. Nothing here was cold, it seemed, except for him. "Here, the local population is a little more...primitive. But for some reason, they seem rather grateful for the employment."

I looked up at his tone. His lips twisted in that crooked smile again, self-loathing evident in the lines of his face. Not aged, exactly, but...fragile, somehow, beneath that marble facade.

"I know what you mean," I said, thinking back to

my arrival in New Orleans, adding to my list of things to ask Minette. "Do you age?" I blurted.

He laughed again. "Yes, I age. You won't see it on the outside, but inside I am...rather broken, I'm afraid. Centuries of living death does that to a— well, I'm not a man any longer, am I?" His mouth twisted again, all his self-deprecating humor slipping from his face.

"You're centuries old?" I whispered, my mind whirling.

His fingers twined in my hair, pulling my head back so my throat lay exposed to him.

"Tell me you're not afraid, Gella."

I swallowed, curling my hands around his arms. "No." My breath hitched, though his increased, puffs hit my skin. "I'm not afraid."

His lips touched my throat, dragging downwards to where my pulse hammered beneath the surface and lingered there. "And now?"

Heat rushed through me at the demanding contact until I slumped in his arms, panting. I remembered the way his hand closed around my throat before, squeezing enough to restrict my breath. Between my legs, swollen flesh throbbed.

"No," I moaned, my voice was ragged. Something far darker than fear rose inside me. I arched against his touch, biting back a whimper.

A light pressure hit the sensitive curve of my neck, and I stifled a whimper. My flesh broke out in a shiver as his teeth pressed harder, the tips breaking the skin.

And now?

"I'm not afraid of you, Sebastian." I curled my hands in his hair, pulling his head down, pressing his teeth deeper against my skin, encouraging him. Pain bloomed around where his lips touched me then numbed, soothing. His tongue dragged across the surface of my throat.

I tipped my head back further, letting my hands drop to his shoulders. My eyes closed, every sense heightening as he supported me, though I could barely feel his lips on my skin. A feral, angry sound ripped from his chest, and his hands were gone.

I fell back onto the bed, dizzy, the room spinning around me. I tried to sit, pushing my elbows back, but his weight bore down on me. I stared up at him, my breaths shallow, desperate for more contact. My entire body craved his touch, as though I were drunk on him.

You see the monster I am, Gella?

The velvet voice in my head dropped away, his tones harsh, abrasive in my mind, but it didn't change my reaction to him. Stubborn, I managed to raise my hands, closing them around his arms. My grip was weak, and when he came to me, it was by his choice, not mine.

"Spread your legs, Gella," he commanded. His voice was laced with authority, and something cold that made me hot all over.

Biting my lip, I widened my thighs until he settled between them, his hard cock resting inside my entrance. The insides of my legs tightened against his hips, but he shook his head.

"Wider," he grated. Sebastian shook his head when I lay frozen beneath him. "Don't make me ask you again."

I spread my legs until my knees ached with the strain.

"Good girl," he murmured, sinking the head of his cock inside me. "Raise your hips, work me with the pretty little body of yours."

I whimpered, but he stayed still and as unmoving as the morning I had woken with him in the library. His expression fathomless, I shivered beneath his granite gaze.

Move your fucking hips, Gella.

I moaned at the intrusion in my mind, already complying. His length slid into me, then out. I lifted myself up again, straining to complete his order. "You're everywhere."

You have no idea.

I cried out as his hand clamped down on my hip, his thumb sliding along the sensitive patch there, claiming me. "Sebastian!"

Without a touch of his teeth to my throat, I fell into a well of bliss so deep, I couldn't see anything but the flame of desire in his eyes.

Then there was nothing.

CHAPTER NINE

GISELLA

I woke alone. The bed was cold, the sun was up, and I was starving. *Two days of faire l'amour with your new husband will do that.* I shifted beneath the heavy quilt, shivering. My feet pressed around to find the brick, but there wasn't one. Sighing, I sat upright, swinging my legs around.

The room swung with me.

I gripped the edges of my bed, waiting for it to slow. I needed food. Sebastian hadn't taken blood from me last night; at least, not that I remembered. Had he? I tried to think back but lost myself in the pleasure of the moment until I couldn't concentrate on anything else. When I found myself in my bed once more, my thighs were slick with arousal. I didn't need to touch myself to know that. As the floor resumed its usual stasis, a pair of black booted feet appeared next to my naked ones.

"Madame, you'll need to eat." Minette propped my shoulders, pushing me back to rest against pillows she fluffed behind me, drawing the sheet up over the swell of my breast in a matron-like fashion.

The tiny woman moved with speed. I settled though the room began to spin again. A hot cup of coffee was pushed into my hands.

I guzzled the sharp liquid, warmth spreading through me from the inside and out, where I clung to the mug with a death grip.

"Sebastian—is he?"

Minette's fussing halted, her face closing down.

"He'll be sleeping, madame. He will rise with the night. As usual."

"He can't wake through the day at all?" I frowned, thinking back to my first day when I'd seen him in the hall, and then the ballroom.

"He can, about an hour after sunrise. But he doesn't often, not usually." Her gaze held mine for a moment, then she resumed her fussing, piling plates around me.

"I can't eat all this. It's far too much," I protested, still attached to my cup. She refilled it, and I smiled, grateful.

"Of course, you will. After all, he took a lot."

He took what? I frowned, thinking back, but the nights were a blur.

Your blood, Gella. What I took from you.

"Oh," I said aloud, still vague. I peered at Minette,

but the maid didn't seem to have heard him. For now, his voice spoke inside my head alone. Perhaps Charleton was the staff member he chose to terrorize in that manner. She returned my smile with thin lips.

I choose to scare Charleton on occasion. A...hobby of mine.

"That's not a nice hobby. Poor man," I muttered under my breath.

Minette frowned at me. "Madame?"

"Nothing." I waved her away, my awkwardness returning along with my embarrassment. She frowned again and retreated, leaving me with a clutch of food and a cup filled to the brim.

Guilt washed over me. Inside my head, Sebastian laughed.

"Don't laugh. They put up with enough from you," I snapped tartly. I had the impression of his disapproval before Sebastian's presence disappeared, and I was left to myself.

By the time I sampled most of the plates, plus refilled my coffee for the umpteenth time, I knew I had to get up or risk sleeping through the day. As much as I wanted to see Sebastian again, I didn't want to replicate his nocturnal habits. Sunlight was still important to me, though I experienced a wave of guilt at sampling its warm pleasures alone.

Is that why you're so cold?

The wayward thought took up residence in my head, but I didn't believe that was his reasoning for not seeing sunlight. Maybe his library would hold more information on the topic. But right now, that wasn't where I wanted to be.

Shifting everything from my bed to the floor, I stood, waiting for the room to start spinning again, but the one thing that dropped was my overfull bladder. As I relieved myself, I made a note to thank Minette—she'd known exactly what to do for me.

How many others had she helped? *Was* there a string of women he fed from, or did he prey on the staff alone? I shuddered at the thought of him as he was last night with me, with another woman—frankly, with anyone else at all.

I waited for his snarky comment as I dressed. Minette had laid out a gorgeous pale-green day dress for me that matched my complexion to perfection. I fingered the scalloped hem, waiting for a response but my headspace remained my own.

I've upset him.

Deeply.

And in turn, that upset me, too.

I wandered through the halls of the upper floor, conspicuously absent of life in any form. No flock of servants assaulted me today. Even the bugs didn't bother me here. The questions I should have asked my husband began to bombard me, instead.

Why wasn't I afraid of him? Why had I adapted to

this life, to a man I'd met days before? My God, I didn't even know what day it *was*.

Why was I not more homesick? I loved France, missed my father, broken man he was. This place seemed so different, though I had been outside for very little time.

Eventually, I found myself pacing the gallery. Sebastian's many faces stared at me through centuries worth of time. How old was he? They must have all been painted before he had relocated—ahh, yet another question to ask my absentee partner.

Why, why, why?

I was never going to be able to hold a significant conversation with him at this rate.

I wandered to the far end of the gallery where the portraits began to show the passage of time. Though my husband still appeared the same, paint crinkled at the aged edges, dust heavy on the frame as though no one dared to clean it, lest it dissipates beneath their hands.

Time, it seemed, was more fragile than the monster it held within.

Heavy drapes lined the windows right to the edge of the hall. What I thought was the end of the hall, until a sprinkle of gold caught my eye. A gilded edge peeked from beneath the drape. I drew it back with caution, not wanting to destroy any further art, but the hall continued a few steps into deep shadow.

Returning to the center of the gallery, I collected a small lamp from the opposite wall—one of many present in each room—and returned to the curtained end of the corridor. Foreboding filled me, but I pressed into the darkness, heedless of the lick of fear that flickered along my spine in a ghostly touch. Sebastian's presence, something older than the man I knew, shrouded around me like a cloak, neither hot nor cold, but lacking in any sort of comfort.

I lifted the lamp to view the hidden portraits. Four descended into the dim light, ending in a dead-end, the final picture facing me but too dark to see. I started at the one to my left, working my way forward.

This painting was much like the others in the gallery. Sebastian stared back at me, his face younger than I had seen before. Rather than the roundness of boyhood or teen years, his face was all angles, lacking in fullness. His eyes set deep, widened, as though in panic.

He looked...starved.

I blinked, uncomfortable beneath the still gaze of his haunted eyes, and moved to the next portrait, lifting the lamp high. This painting was set in deep reds and blacks, his flesh stark, lifeless against the open collar of his shirt. His face drawn, he appeared the same age as in the prior painting.

But his eyes—those dark orbs that pinned me in place as he taught my body how to please his, those held a tinge of demonic red, piercing as though they tracked my every step. I blinked, backing up a pace, and collided with a very warm body.

The lamp tumbled from my fingers.

"Oh!"

A startled Charleton dived to catch it, landing on the plush carpet, the glass cupped in his pale hands.

"Nicely saved," I observed, pressing my palms to my skirts. "Thank you."

"You're welcome. But—you really shouldn't be here." He gripped my elbow in a tight grip, towing me around.

I shook myself free with a frown. "I wasn't finished." I reached for the lamp, but he pulled it away. "Charleton. The lamp, please."

"It's nearly luncheon. You must be famished."

"I'm not. Minette overfed me at breakfast. I must thank the cook later." My hand still held out for the lamp, I raised an encouraging eyebrow.

"And you haven't seen the grounds. Let me take you on a tour." Desperation entered his voice, which heightened my curiosity.

"The lamp."

Charleton paused in his efforts, resignation drawing his features tight across his weary face. "Madame, I must insist…"

"Noted."

This time, when I reached for the lamp, he let me take it. I nodded my thanks, unsmiling. Without over-thinking it, I gripped the lamp tight and strode back to the end of the hall, halting before the portrait hanging at the end, facing me.

Light bloomed on something that should have remained hidden. I stepped back from the scarlet eyes that showed horror beyond measure in their depths. A scream lodged in my throat as I traced over Sebastian's younger self. *This* was what he had become when his humanity had...deserted him.

Red skin flayed raw captured a face more demonic than mortal, like something that should never have come to the surface had been released here, and seeing the light of day, crawled back into the darkness from where it had emerged. Thin flesh pressed to his bones, as though his body was dying but his mind refused to release him from this life. He was quite unrecognizable, except for the smile.

The twisted, ruined smile that was all Sebastian, and the man I knew.

A pair of eyes stared from behind his mangled face —eyes I knew quite well, had been on the ship with for months while we transited across the Atlantic from France to America. I stepped closer, peering into the shadow behind Sebastian's death mask.

Amy's sweet, perfect face stared back at me.

For the second time that morning, I dropped the lamp.

Are you satisfied, Gella? Are you frightened now?

Sebastian's enraged voice echoed around the gallery. Hate emanated from the picture as heat pooled around my feet.

I screamed as hands grasped my shoulders, yanking me backward. Landing on my backside with an undignified thump, I watched Charleton smother the lamp with his coat. He stamped at embers escaping the edges, though the carpet seemed disinclined to ignite, smoldering with faint wisps of smoke that rose from his charred jacket.

When the last flame died, Charleton hunched over his knees, propping himself up with his hands. He wiped a smoke-stained cuff over his brow, decorating his face reddened with exertion and soot.

"I'm so sorry, Charleton," I whispered. "I should have listened to you."

He swung toward me. Not an ounce of anger strained his face, though bone-deep exhaustion marked the hollows of his eyes.

The sole emotion he aimed at me was pity. And after seeing who my husband was, who he had been... I would take every ounce directed my way.

And his.

Though I knew he'd hate me forever for seeing him that way.

CHAPTER TEN

SEBASTIAN

I knew I would break her, but I didn't know how much it would fucking hurt.

The monster in me craved the fear and self-loathing I'd become accustomed to coming my way whenever I ventured into society. But this was different. This time, I cared, and I wasn't prepared for the dose of the first from her, and the second from myself.

I deserve every inch of her hatred.

"I don't hate you. I'm just scared of you. Right now, anyway."

I blinked at her whispered admission that was meant for me alone, hissed into her lace handkerchief away from Charleton's shivering form.

Such a brave little prey, I mocked her, digging the dose of self-hatred deeper. *Did you think I was the tame sort of monster created to warm your mortal bed and slink away with the sunrise?*

Don't do that.

Her reply seared directly into my mind.

I jerked back mentally with an oath, and closed the connection, blocking her out, if only for a short period. I knew I wouldn't be able to stay away from her for long. Ironic that she'd become the addiction I craved, and now she'd etched herself into my blood, an intangible brand that claimed me as much as I claimed her.

Only I was the monster within, not her.

Are we not the same?

Her voice floated through my consciousness, but I wasn't certain if this version was my imagination. But the sense of persistence, of not giving up that swept over me sure as fuck wasn't from me. The dead part of me wanted to smile as I envisioned her giving Charleton a talking to, while the other part of me found decrepit ways to punish my little wife for her transgressions.

The longer I remained motionless, the worse my retribution became in my head, though I doubted I would do little more than turn her pretty, pale behind pink before I fucked us both into the sort of oblivion I enjoyed. The sort with no other voice in my head.

Won't you let me play with her?

The ghost of my sins followed me from place to place, haunting my death as she ruined my life. In no way would I let her stain the burgeoning emotion I discovered with my new wife.

In such a short time I'd found a human with whom I could co-exist, who stayed with me not because of a skewed sense of loyalty, like Charleton did, or the payment the servants took for their families, or a reminder, a remnant of their homeland. No, Gisella seemed to actually like me for *me*.

Until now.

I groaned in my head and wondered if she heard that too, experienced my consternation alongside me. Or, if like all the others, she only discovered the void of the soul I no longer possessed, frittered away on beauty that was skin deep, at absolute best.

My ruminations turned inward, as always. What was one to spend their deathly hours upon, if not a little self-sabotage? The soulless, like myself, never had the perfect nothingness of sleep. Even dreams would be better than the endless hours of memories of too many years. A man was never designed to live an eternal life, and for good reason.

A sleepless life of eternal memory and less forgiveness drove a mind to madness.

And now that Gisella had seen that part of me, would she forgive my monster? Certainly, she'd seen me take from her, had experienced it herself. But the evil I held within...she saw it displayed, flayed and raw and born again like a twisted branch of a cultish religion and her the altar I worshipped at.

If she didn't run during the daylight hours, perhaps she would at night. A smile teased the corners of my dead lips. It had been so long since I hunted. And tasting her fear...

A snarl ripped at my mind inside. *Not her.*

She tasted too fucking good. I'd never stop, ripping her apart until, even if her body survived by some miracle, her mind I'd shatter with the pure force of my own.

And some decrepit, monstrous part of me craved her submission in every way, wondering just how much of my pain and hatred my pretty little wife would endure for me.

The hours before sunset melded my hunger and arousal into a hideous thing until even death struggled to contain me.

And when I couldn't be contained any longer, I'd come for her.

CHAPTER ELEVEN

GISELLA

Charleton escorted me along the hall, jacket still smoldering on the gallery's carpet. He drew the heavy drapes with disdain, as though he couldn't have cared less if the entire gallery went up in flames.

So much for *protect the portraits.*

To my surprise, Charleton led me to the front door. A twinge started in my belly, panic spreading quickly.

I clasped my hands together, willing my voice steady. "Am I being evicted?" Proud of the evenness in my voice, I even managed to accompany it with a small smile.

Celebrate the small things, Gella.

Sebastian's harsh voice grated on my nerves. That I'd done something wrong by him, and Charleton, the people who had let me into their lives when I was but an insurgent into their established lives, an outsider, that ruined something important inside me that I had clung to, and not known.

Your trust.

A huff answered me, though no new words entered my head. Sebastian left me alone with my own thoughts. To my horror, a tear escaped down my cheek.

Charleton drew me into the sunlight on the broad drive, overlooking the forest below. "This is your home, as it is ours." The butler-cum-valet turned me to face him. "We serve our master because we are bound to him. He gave us a home, the safety of this place. That bond is stronger than any piece of paper. You also are bound, but your freedom is your own. I'm sure he would agree." Anger rose in his face for the first time, as though daring Sebastian to dispute his offer.

If he doesn't like that, I'm sure we will both hear about it.

Both of us paused, waiting, but there was nothing the man in question added to our weird conversation.

"I don't want to leave," I blurted. "I want to wait for him to—" I swallowed the tears that threatened, but in the end, there were too many. They cascaded down my cheeks, and I lost myself too deep in self-pity to care.

"I'm sure he will see you tonight." Charleton withdrew a clean hankerchief, pressing it into my hands. I clung to it, much as I had my cup this morning. "Why don't you sit in the sun until he wakes? I'll send Minette for company—in fact, I think we could all use a little sunlight right now." A smile entered Charleton's voice.

I nodded, cleaning myself off. "Please. I would be grateful."

"As we are to you, madame." He bowed low, gesturing me to the entrance to the gardens off of the drive, and returned to the darkness of the house.

I frowned after him, wondering what he meant. The gate to the gardens was covered with climbing plants I didn't recognize. An archway cut into the high hedge held a kissing gate that led from the drive. The place had a lived-in quality the rest of the estate lacked, from the forbidding forest to the closed-in house. I leaned on the gate, and it swung outward. I stepped through the hedge, letting the gate swing closed behind me.

Walking through Sebastian's gardens was like stepping across oceans and into my home province. Fragrant roses edged the lush green hedges. Sprays of lavender were surrounded by the quiet humming of bees nestled in the flowers.

A small flagstone pathway lined with irises led to a large, formal fountain. Water tumbled from the lips of a gothic creature, its limbs twisted and contorted with a comical expression, not unlike the gargoyles which often adorned the rooflines of churches and buildings in Paris.

He was an oddly comforting companion, despite his repulsive appearance. I scooped up my skirts, settling on the fountain's wide-lipped edge. Water splashed around me, offering a gentle relief from the warmth of the day, past its height.

Voices and a clatter of footsteps turned my head. Minette led a gaggle of downstairs staff into the garden. Armed with blankets and baskets, they laid out a picnic lunch with a degree of efficiency I envied. I knelt to grab a corner of a bright red rug, straightening it. Minette shooed me away with an expression of abject horror, but I shook my head, determined to be more than a useless figure amongst the flurry of activity around me.

As people settled on the blankets, piled with plates and a lemony drink that was somehow both sweet and sour, I was astounded to count the staff employed by the estate. And, knowing some aspect must be farmed or worked in an outdoor capacity, this wouldn't be the full capacity Sebastian employed, all keeping his secrets.

"Did you empty the house?" I asked Minette softly.

Beside me, a maid and her beau chattered in soft undertones, their frequent touches a comforting sight. *All love is not lost here.* No, in true French fashion, flirtation and romance were heady in the air, reminding me of a slice of home. Charleton sat with another young man, discussing finer points of dressing their employer. I was glad to see he had replaced his ruined coat with a fresh one, overhearing his passionate discussion with the younger man. I shook my head. Even when he didn't need to be working, he couldn't stop. Minette's eyes followed his companion's enthused conversation, and I wondered if this was the elusive James.

"I thought you might like the company." Her soft smile lit up her entire, heart-shaped face. The expression froze as she glanced at the house and then back to me. "I—I hope I didn't overstep my bounds, madame."

"Not at all." I returned her smile. "I'm glad for the company. Especially after... Will Charleton forgive me?" I kept my tone light, but a knot tightened in my stomach at the reminder of this morning's debacle. "And please, call me Gisella. This isn't that sort of place, it seems."

If they forgive me for breaking their rules.

Will Sebastian?

"Of course, he will. It was bound to happen sometime. Or something of the sort." Minette busied herself, piling my plate with sausage and beignets.

"Why do you stay here? Knowing what I do of... Sebastian." I blinked as his presence filled my mind, as though the mere mention of his name might summon him.

She shrugged a light shoulder. "James and I came from a plantation estate to the north. They treated people...poorly, there." Her smile was haunted, and I knew that wasn't half the story. "Many come to newer towns to escape something they've left behind— ruined families, war service, other...forms of employment. It's a new start for every person here. His lordship ignored all those things and gave each of us clothes, a safe place to sleep each night. Food. We give him..." Her mouth set in a line, though it wasn't hard this time, and she shrugged again.

I poked at the sausage as she added dainty puffs of cooked batter to my plate, my mind awhirl with the information and what on earth I was to do with it. The household was a broken collection of dolls, and I was no exception, lacking the glue to hold us all together. Pastry flaked around my fingers as I pressed too hard on the sides of the cloud-like puff.

"What's this?"

"Try it." She smiled mysteriously.

I bit into the puff. A savory explosion of flavor burst across my tongue, the soft center warring with the crisp outer shell. "That's delicious. What is it?"

"Fried oyster." Minette continued to pile my plate high until I held up my hands to stop her.

"Who do I have to thank for this magnificent feast?"

"Desiree," Minette called. A rotund, tanned woman scooted across the rug to join us. "Ma—Gisella," she caught herself and sent a rueful grin in my direction, "wanted to compliment you on your food."

Desiree's face lit up. "You enjoyed it?"

A lilt lifted her words in a sing-song tone.

I nodded, grinning. "You're responsible for breakfast this morning, too?"

Desiree nodded, stuffing a beignet into her mouth.

Enjoying yourself?

I smiled outwardly, hiding my surprise at Sebastian's easy tone behind the facade of drinking.

Trying to fit in with the normal crowd?

I blinked, his anger rolling over me. I'd assumed wrong. "Not now," I muttered under my breath.

"Beg your pardon?" Minette asked, her brow furrowing as she stared at me.

I placed the cup back onto the blanket. "Excuse me." I rose, straightening my skirts, and paced through the low, hip-high hedges, moving away from the small crowd gathered at the garden entrance.

I'm glad you made time for me.

His mocking voice roiled around my head in a snarl I could envision written across his handsome face all too well.

"What's got you riled?" I asked softly, curling loose strands of hair around my fingers to cover my mouth, though I already knew what had upset him.

My staff don't appear to be doing their job.

"But they are doing a job. And they're doing it wonderfully."

What job is that?

His anger rocked me again.

I stopped walking. "They're giving me a reason not to leave. They're giving me a home, Sebastian. Like you have given to them."

Silence saturated our strained conversation, leaving a deep void between us. I swallowed, continuing to wind my way through the hedges which grew taller the deeper I ventured into the garden.

"Sebastian?" I traced the line of shadows with my feet where they began to merge in the late afternoon. "I don't want to leave."

Nothing.

I sighed, walking around a corner, and found myself in the middle of a wide, open space, paved with colored tiles—a child's mosaic. Circular paths branched away from it in all directions. I turned to retrace my steps but found myself with too many options. The paved tiles gave no indication of which branch I'd come from.

I stared between them, bearing down on a small wave of panic. Which path took me back to the gathering? I peered back across the labyrinth of hedges, but I couldn't even see the ugly stone gargoyle. In my conversation with Sebastian, I had wandered far distant from the group, almost to the edge of the forest.

The shadow of the castle stood close to my slippered feet. I edged back as it crept closer, like long fingers reaching for me.

I'm glad you want to stay.

Sebastian's voice intruded on my deliberations, swiping aside my fear.

Am I interrupting you again, my wife?

"No, of course not," I answered, distracted by the choices before me. I trotted down one path to be brought back to the center of the courtyard I had started in a moment before, and no closer to my goal. Another choice led me to the same outcome. "Um, how do I get out of your maze?"

What are you doing in there? Never mind. Follow the red poppies. They'll lead you back to the gate.

I breathed a gusty sigh, relief lessening the line of

tension in my shoulders I hadn't known I carried. "Thank you." Another thought occurred to me. "Will you tell me about Amy?"

Another pause. I located a row of red poppies and followed the path. This one didn't turn back on itself, offering me a short respite.

I'll see you tonight, Gella.

I rolled my eyes. My new husband was never one not to be enigmatic, it seemed. I promised myself I'd ask all the questions I needed tonight. *And* get the answers, too, though I knew he wouldn't make those easy. I smiled to myself, likely looking like a loon as I traipsed away from the looming shadows for a brief respite.

Until I took a wrong turn.

The red poppies turned to whites, then a dusky purple. In the deepening shadows, they became more difficult to pick out. Finally, the petals turned black. I groaned, lifting my skirts to my ankles, trotting in ever quicker steps. The shadows deepened, melding the rows together as the sun hung above the horizon. The end of the path appeared to open out ahead. I picked up my pace, though the staff were likely long gone.

Huffing, I reached the end, and stepped onto a slippery tile. Skidding a little, I flailed for balance as the sun sank out of sight, daylight succumbing to a dusky twilight, back in the center of the mosaic I thought I had long left behind.

Lost.

CHAPTER TWELVE

GISELLA

I turned back in the direction from where I had come, but I could barely see the poppies, let alone discern their color in the failing dusk. A scream of frustration edged with panic lodged in my throat. I swallowed it down, refusing to let a simple garden maze overcome me.

Follow the poppies, indeed. I shook my head, hoping for more instructions, but Sebastian was nowhere in my head. Stepping towards one of the paths, I bent down, running my hand over the tops of plants. Soft petals brushed my hand. All I had to do was follow them.

Follow, follow, follow.

Such a simple task. Clenching my stomach, I refused to allow the impending panic rise higher. This had to be the right choice, I told myself firmly. The hedges loomed above me as I strode along the path, my quick pace reducing my short pants by a minor amount. Progress meant finding everyone who no doubt thought I'd wandered off at their master's bidding.

Heart hammering, I took a turn at a row of dark poppies, or at least, what I thought were poppies, then another. Finally, I arrived at a forked section of the maze I didn't recognize and took the left-hand path.

Without the sun to guide me I was guessing, but in the back of my mind, doubt seeded.

"Stupid, stupid," I muttered to myself.

I trotted on between the hedges that seemed to close in on me. Small, waxy leaves brushed my fingers. Snapped twigs caught on my skirts. I trotted faster, breaking into an outright run until the hedge opened out into a broad space. My gait slowed as I blinked into the darkness.

Water bubbled nearby, and I almost ran to the fountain in my relief. The gargoyle stood tall, his bulky arms raised. Cold air shifted around me, and I turned to see the castle rising dark and forbidding against the starlit sky.

A void of its own, stealing the light. Relief washed over me. At least I knew where I was, now. I walked around the fountain, then paused, studying the gargoyle. His arms were twisted, muscular, a more masculine shape than I pictured earlier in the day.

I frowned, recalling his shape as hunched, bent. But then, I hadn't walked around this side of the fountain. Well, I *had*, but Sebastian and I were arguing at the time, and I doubted I would have noticed much at all. The craftsmanship of the creature was incredible. Whoever had carved him had created the face perfectly—the right mixture of handsome and grotesque in perfect symmetry.

"If you're done staring." The face moved, but I couldn't reconcile it with the voice—until the gargoyle lowered his hands. I shook my head, retreating a step, but he followed me, peering down. "It is quite rude, you know."

My mouth stretched wide, I sucked in a lung full of air, retreating in a flurry of steps while I tried to remind my voice how to scream.

You told me no other monsters were in your lands!

Another unanswered plea. I should be used to them by now.

I tripped over my own feet, stumbling back into something hard, unforgiving. A hand wrapped around my mouth. The water stopped running, and all I could hear in the garden was the echo of my silenced scream.

"Gisella. Gella, stop."

The hand squeezed my chin gently, forcing my head back in a slow movement. I shook my head, but the hand kept me still until I was looking up into a pair of dark eyes I'd last seen above me the night before.

"Don't fight me, hellion," he murmured, reducing my fear with a single phrase.

Sebastian held my gaze a moment longer, then

nodded, lowering his hand. Turning me in his arms, he tightened his grasp, pulling me against him.

I closed my eyes tight, certain I was safe with him.

That's not something I ever expected to hear from you again.

"Then you should keep out of other people's heads," I muttered tartly into the folds of his shirt.

Sebastian laughed deeply, slipping his fingers beneath my bonnet into my hair, holding me tight. *Safe.* "Dolion. About time you got up. But truly, man, did you need to scare her? She'd been lost for hours by the time I woke." He spoke over my head.

A deep voice answered him, and I stiffened, pressing deeper into Sebastian's chest. He squeezed my back with one hand—his almost fit almost all the way across my slight frame.

"I did see her go into the maze, earlier. If I'd known she was lost, I would have brought her out myself."

I peeked over my shoulder, my body pressed thigh to thigh with Sebastian's. A man's silhouette graced the moonlight behind me. Sebastian's arms flexed again, releasing me when I gave a gentle nudge to the confines of his embrace. I turned to face the man who had been a monster.

Everything about him was the same—the carved muscle, the shape of his body, his bulk—but absent was the twisted, grotesque facial expression. Instead, his was one of kindness, with a mischievous light in his yellow eyes. The stone of his body reflected golden skin, gleaming as though oiled beneath the moon.

I swallowed, attempting a watery smile.

You promised me no more monsters.

I sent the reminder to the alabaster statue of a man of my own at my back, receiving a soft huff of breath I was convinced he didn't need against my nape. Shivers broke out across my arms. I folded my hands in front of me, trying to suppress the cold that seeped into my body. A broad arm wrapped tight around my chest, pulling me back into him, his coat offering warmth when his body couldn't.

"I am sorry." The gargoyle's—*Dolion*—voice rumbled deep and smooth, as though dipped in honey. "I get bored there, alone while you have your fun. It's not like I can jump down and join in, yes?" He smiled as he straightened, heavy, bunched muscles turning lean. Standing tall, his height was intimidating, even against Sebastian.

"No, I suppose not," I murmured, reaching for my husband's hand, tangling my fingers tight in his when I located it.

He squeezed back, his other arm returning to my waist.

"Out for the night, then?" Above me, Sebastian's voice held a hint of meaning, though he covered it well with a casual tone.

"All night, brother. Playing with the old woman's wolves." The stone turned man flashed a smile my way before he leaped through the garden with impossible speed, fading into the shadows and out of my sight.

Sebastian's palm pressed against my stomach, his

fingers caressing the gentle swell there. With Dolion gone, we were left alone in the garden, well sheltered from the view of the house. Slowly, he turned me in his arms to face him. My mouth dry, I swallowed back a different sort of fear that trembled through me at the change in his touch.

His gaze darkened as his fingers caught my chin, tipping my head up. With deft fingers, he removed my bonnet, tossing the confection of lace and straw aside. His hand returned to my hair, tangling in the loosened strands.

I pressed my fingers to his cool chest, straying over the curves and valleys there. "Sebastian—"

He pulled me closer, his breath almost kissing my lips. If I leaned up on my tiptoes, my mouth would meet his, and I knew what would happen the moment he kissed me. The passion between us became a tangible thing that wound us ever tighter in its embrace.

I closed my eyes as my heart raced.

Please, kiss me.

Don't kiss me and take me inside.

But as frightening as the garden had become, swathed in shadows and dark corners when I had traversed it on my own, it was a place of peace with Sebastian before me, because I knew that above everything else, he would protect me.

I'd been wrong to fight with him, to run from him. There were all sorts of monsters in this world, and not all of them drank blood or died at first light. My hands curled into fists on his shirt, tugging him closer and pushing away at the same time.

"I will never tell you to leave me, Gella," he growled against my lips before his mouth came crashing down on mine.

Tongue and teeth tangled in a clash of need. I reached around his neck to twist my fingers in his hair, tugging on the dark waves. He groaned into my mouth, his hardness pressing against my stomach. The night passed over us while he bruised my lips and devoured my mouth. When he drew back, my mind and body were still whirling with emotion—both mine and his.

"Why does that happen?" I murmured, dragging dozy eyelids open.

"Because you're insatiable," he answered, a gleam in his dark eyes.

I nudged him in the ribs with my fingers, but he didn't so much as *oof*. Typical. "Not that. I mean, why do I get what you're feeling?"

Sebastian drew back sharply. "What do you mean?"

I shrugged, uncomfortable to be under his scrutiny again. "When you spoke to me in the garden, I could feel your anger, your rage at being...well, at not being able to join us. And now," I flapped lamely. "I shouldn't have said anything."

"Of course, you should." He tucked me into his shoulder, drawing me along the path that led back into the garden.

"I just came from here," I protested, "Maybe we could go back to the house?"

"The house has ears." He tightened his grip on my arm.

Stubborn man.

"And your garden has eyes," I retorted. "Is anything else going to jump out at me? Wait—your stone man—"

"Dolion."

"Yes. He said there are wolves." I shivered involuntarily at the thought of sharp teeth and found I couldn't face the image.

"Not...natural ones."

I took a moment to ponder that. "You didn't say native," I murmured.

"No. I didn't." He laughed, a cruel, twisted sound. "I told you I'm the monster here."

"So you say," I grumbled, amazed at my own acceptance.

Or maybe it was him. I shivered despite his hold on me.

The shadows have eyes.

I'd never call my thoughts fanciful ever again.

"You're safe with me, Gella. I won't let you be lost again."

"Your directions were dreadful," I offered, to break the tension.

"Perhaps you didn't follow them correctly."

"Perhaps," I echoed softly.

Perhaps you couldn't find your way around a map with both hands.

Sebastian laughed again, though true humor

coated the deep sound this time. Flashes of the day ran back to me—his portrait, the fire. Amy. A tremor ran over my shoulders at the thought of her, my mind whirling at the connotations I hadn't taken the time to process.

His arm tightened around me. "Gella?"

"I set fire to your gallery."

He harrumphed into my hair, dropping a kiss to the top of my head. "I know." He sounded resigned, as though he knew what was coming.

I barreled ahead anyway.

"Tell me about Amy."

He walked in silence for a few minutes, drawing me deeper into the gardens, along the hedgerow. My teeth chattered. I didn't want to go back into the maze. Glancing over my shoulder, light framed the curtained windows of the house, warm and welcoming. Despite my need to escape its confines earlier in the day, all I wanted now was to be back within those four impenetrable walls.

At the entrance to the maze, Sebastian steered us to one side, through a grove of trees I hadn't noticed in my haste before. The slim trees were planted in a circle. Moss covered the ground, squishing beneath my feet. He didn't stop in the clearing but instead led me through the other side, dropping his arm to clasp my hand.

We slipped between the close-knit, twisted trees and stepped out onto a wide ledge that ended in a little shoal looking out across the ocean. Water lapped softly in the muggy air, as tepid as a long-standing teacup, like I imagined from his bedroom. I glanced over my shoulder to see if I could pick his out, but foliage obscured my sight of the house.

When I turned back, he led me to a wide, rectangular slab of rock that rested to one side of the sandy space. His head inclined, he gestured for me to sit. I spread my skirts around me and waited. Sebastian paced before me, treading a worn path he seemed to know well.

"Amy—I know her as Anitta. It's an older name." He ran his hand over his head, smoothing loose strands away from his face that sprang back in a show of defiance. "She's different. Not like me, older than Dolion. My gargoyle. She predates us all."

I blinked. How many creatures of the night were there? But not all legends stayed hidden under the cover of darkness while innocents only dreamed of the magic that created them.

I frowned. "But she was in the sunlight. On the ship. And she—she didn't sleep. Not like you, when you...you know, in the morning..." I waved a feeble hand.

"She is not vampyre, Gella."

It was the first time he had said that word to me, and imparting the knowledge, voicing it—it was an offering of trust.

I'll never ask you to leave, Gella. You have my promise.

And I'll never run from you.

The two-way conversation ran over my words. I considered for a moment.

"What is she? She's lived all these years, my God, centuries—" I paused as he winced. "What is it?"

"Please refrain from mentioning Him, love."

"Oh." I quietened. "Do—should I not cross myself, then?"

He laughed. "No, love. Gestures like that hold no power whatsoever. His name, however, regardless of form, does."

"You avoided my question." My mind caught up with me. I raised an eyebrow in his direction. "Again."

"I'm getting good at that," he mused, studying the stars.

"Yes." I jabbed him again, though it wasn't a satisfying barb without earning a reaction. "You are."

Sebastian sighed, slowing his pace. "She is—I don't know what she is, only who. She found me when I was...killed. Alive. How ever you wish to say it." He laughed, a hollow thing that sent shivers across my flesh.

I crossed my arms tightly. Chill night air seeped through my dress. He glanced down at me and slipped out of his coat, laying it around my shoulders. For the first time, I recognized that he had a scent. Something fresh—like dew on a frosted morning, mixed with the earthy undertones of charcoal and smoke.

"When were you..." I bit my lip, unsure if it was polite to ask someone when they were killed.

Sebastian laughed again, but there was no humor

in it. "When did I die?" The laughter inside him held for a moment before it crashed, sinking into something dark, suppressed deep, and mirrored in his eyes. "Four hundred years ago. She was there when my body changed, like I was flayed from the inside out."

I stifled a gasp behind my hand. "The portrait."

He didn't look at me this time. "Yes. The portrait. She was there. Watched me from the inside."

Reveled in it.

His silent confession imparted the horror he didn't dare to say aloud.

"Like we talk? Inside my head?"

"You're inside mine, too, Gella," he murmured.

"Oh." Disconcerted at the thought of my voice talking in his head, though I supposed it made sense, I thought back to my time on the ship. Sharing a cabin with her. "Does that mean she might be in my head, too? Amy, I mean?"

He looked down with a furrowed brow. "Why would you say that?"

"Well, because we were on the ship for so long, and we shared a cabin for the first part of the journey, and —well, we had a few nights I can't quite remember," I mumbled the last part, heat climbing into my cheeks.

"You got drunk?" His voice held constrained laughter, and I was glad to bring a little humor back to him, despite the cost to my ego.

I cleared my throat. "On the rare occasion of a few nights," I lied. "I wondered if," I barreled ahead, "if she might have done something? I don't know, but you keep saying I'm not afraid of you and I should be, but I'm not—" I rambled, cutting myself off. I closed my eyes, shaking my head. None of it made sense. "I shouldn't have said anything." My hands trembled, and I tucked them out of sight beneath his coat.

"Yes." He stared straight ahead, considering. I held my breath, unsure where this train of thought would lead us. "I am surprised you allow me to touch you, having seen me as I truly am. Raw. Evil."

"You're not evil," I said softly.

"Am I not?" he barked, sliding a hand beneath his coat to grip my waist, pulling me to him with a jerk.

A cry tore from me as I clung to his shoulders by reflex, unwilling to fall into the murky, reptile-inhabited waters. Thick, tepid air covered us in a layer of sticky salt, reminding me how far from civilization we were, who I stood with. I curled my hands into his shirt, fisting the material.

"No," I whispered. My heart raced, pressed close to his still one. "Not to me."

"Last night, I tore you open. I *took* from you, Gella. Without any form of consent." His mouth lowered, and he spoke with his lips pressed to my temple. "And I *enjoyed it.* I terrorize the staff. I've taken you from your home."

A roughened knuckle notched below my chin, forcing me to look up into his eyes. I glimpsed the points of his teeth behind his deceptively soft, arched lips.

"I have no home," I corrected him. "My father sold

me to someone he didn't know, by royal proxy. And oddly enough, the staff do like you. All of them. Minette mentioned something about saving them and giving them a place to love and care for. And I—I wanted you to—take from me. Last night." I bit my lip, looking down at my hands scrunched in his shirt, unable to hold his gaze.

"You wanted me to?" Refusing to be deterred, up came the hand again, clenching around my jaw in a firm, but not painful grip. Desire and hunger warred in his gaze, held at bay, if only by the barest tether. Dark eyes searched mine, the night hiding him from me. His breath brushed my lips that tingled in response. Being so close to him did odd things to my body. "Tell me you want that again, Gella."

Jagged, dual bolts of need and fear coursed through my body. I said nothing as he flicked the borrowed coat from my shoulders, leaving them bare in the open neckline of my dress. His mouth touched the corner of my lips, trailing from my jaw to my neck.

A clash of sensation assailed me as I leaned into his touch, offering the consent he craved. In silent agreement, his fingers tangled in my hair, tugging my head to the side to expose my pulse to him.

Eyes closed, I wound my hands around his shoulders, taking comfort and no small degree of pleasure in his nearness. Having him so close was dizzying. I rested my head in his hands and waited for the sting on my skin, still tender and raw from his last feeding.

Sebastian hesitated over the mark he'd left, his

tongue flicking across my pulse. Heat rushed over me in a prickle of anticipation. Again, the numbing sensation settled into me, soaking deep as his bite pierced my skin. I gripped his arms tight through his shirt, pain and bliss sweeping through me in a heady rush.

Lost in a swarm of voices and memories, I swayed where I sat. His arms tightened around me, holding me up. I was glad of his support in the next second when the ground whirled beneath me. I squeezed my eyes tight, holding onto him, but my hands came up empty. The swirling ground slowed.

I opened my eyes to find the garden gone.

CHAPTER THIRTEEN

GISELLA

In place of the boiling seas and Sebastian's dark head, his lips pressed to my skin in an act as intimate as sex, I stood in the cabin I shared on board the ship with Amy without him. A second passed, and another, until his presence faded, leaving me alone with my friend.

The same dim light, the same broken lantern. Warped floorboards rocked beneath my boots in a familiar motion as I crossed the small room, swaying, but the roll of the ship had little to do with my lack of stability.

"You could out drink half the whores in Paris," Amy giggled behind me. I spun, the room taking my stomach on a round the world tour with it. Amy grabbed my arm, holding a bottle of dark liquor under my nose. "Go on. Have another, whore."

She doubled over, giggles consuming her, but

something about the scene felt horribly wrong. Or maybe it was my stomach. I liberated the bottle, swigging from its smooth glass neck all the same. Dark golden liquid burned my tongue and throat on its way down, but a pleasant, spicy ginger taste resided in my mouth afterward.

"What would you know about whores, girl?" I slurred the words, twirling in a dance that took me to the bed.

Warmth trailed along my chest, lack of clean, fresh air clung to the stale breath in my throat. Staring at the ceiling, I watched shadows lengthen and merge across the exposed beams of the ship.

"A whole lot more than you, stuffed away in your nunnery," she pouted.

"English." I shook my head haughtily. "Always think you know everything."

"Maybe we do." Amy poured more of the liquid into me.

I blinked at the shadows as they performed their never-ending dance, warring and merging against the rush of the ship upon the open ocean roaring in my ears.

Amy's lips brushed my ears. "But you'll be the whore, soon enough. He'll love you, want you. Care for you." Her voice filled with venom. The shadows above me danced in a frenzy of limbs, their dance filled with desire and passion. "You'll let me into his house so I can take everything, destroy everything he wants, and leave him with nothing. Like he left me."

I blinked, my lips numb, but I had no words to give her. Figures swarmed across the ceiling, scorching the wood there black with an eternity of sins, and I fell into its eternal darkness.

~

"Gella," Sebastian hissed, withdrawing his lips from my neck.

I blinked. The overheated cabin air was replaced with the bite of the ocean air, fresh and sharp. His hands clutched me tight to him as I swayed where I still sat on the rocky bench, the roll of the sands alive beneath my feet.

He swore above my head, a string of words in a language I didn't understand. The air around us charged with the promise of violence in his voice. His mouth glistened dark and shadowed as he stood over me, somehow more imposing than before. Looking up at him was like staring into the face of a dark, vengeful god. His gaze dropped to me, his hooded eyes those of a hunter.

For the first time, I was afraid.

I pressed back, pushing against his hands, but they wound around me, unyielding. My heart racing, I struggled in his grip, but only succeeded in drawing his attention back to my throat. He dipped his head, and I shrieked, my mind jamming as I knew what would come. A ripping, tearing in a beast-like manner that would end my life here, near the muddied waters of nothingness. Maybe my body would end up taken below the sands by one of the creatures, the damage he did to me indistinguishable.

Despite my fear his touch was light, licking, sucking. Soothing, not hurting. I trembled with fear and shock in his hold, my mind still convinced he would kill me while my body fought to trust the man who had more than proven his worth.

After a time, he drew back, his lips clean, and bent his forehead to mine. "I'm sorry, Gella."

I nodded against him, confused. "What are you sorry for?"

"That she was inside you."

"What?"

"The blackness. You were right. You should have been afraid. Your body should have reacted the way it does now. She's hidden something from you—from me. I can't see it, but whatever she put there, it's not—it isn't you."

My mouth dried. "What do you mean, it isn't me? What part of me?"

Pity consumed his gaze, and I hated it, pulling away from him. He let me go. "The part of you that accepts me, I suspect. She made you want to love me, Gella."

"No. *No.* I—" I searched my mind, running over my feelings for him. I wanted this, the assurance of his safety, his protection. I wanted to feel this way about him, and taking that away...tears sprang to my eyes, tumbling over my lashes in a cascade of grief for something I hadn't lost yet. "*Non.*"

His smile was sad as he dropped his hands and turned away. I waited for whatever would come next, staring up at his broad back, but he said nothing at all. Finally, he took a step forward, away from me.

"Wait, Sebastian— Are you telling me to leave?" A sob tore from my throat.

You promised me.

He paused, his back to me. Moonlight shrouded his silhouette against the dark of the forest beyond.

"Not yet. Follow the path. It will take you to the house."

He hesitated a second longer, his head turning a fraction in my direction. Then he strode away, disappearing deep into the forest where I couldn't follow, leaving me alone at the edge of the garden.

My feet took the path he'd indicated without my permission. I watched the ground as I walked, my slippers covered in dark stains. The night quietened around me, sinking into the depths of hours when even the night animals paused and hid away.

My fingers brushed stone limply. I stopped beside the still fountain and sank onto the wide, sandstone lip. I didn't know how long I sat there, night air numbing my skin, much as he had done before he bit me. I willed tears to come but there was nothing inside me. I was as numb inside, it appeared, as I was on the surface.

Empty, like him.

"He'll return with the night." A voice spoke over my shoulder.

I blinked slowly, wondering if I had turned to stone like the gargoyle perched behind me.

"Will he?" My voice was rough. I swallowed. "He wants me to leave, Dolion."

Light began to brighten the sky in the false dawn, though the sun wouldn't rise for more than an hour.

"He doesn't know what he wants." The gargoyle seated himself beside me, stone lightening his darker natural hues. I wondered if his change came with the impending dawn, like Sebastian's imposed sleep, or if it was his choice. His was a cool, gray stone, which contrasted with the golden hues of the sandstone fountain.

"You were—" I halted, unsure of what sort of term to use, "um, made? By someone other than the fountain." I frowned, knowing I'd messed it up. "I'm so sorry, I don't know how to ask…"

Dolion laughed, a deep bellow that bounced around the courtyard. "It's fine, *petite lynx*. You are new to the world." Depths reflected in his eyes.

I canted my head, looking deeper. It wasn't America he was talking about. "How old are you?" I whispered.

"I was born when the Khan became Emperor of the East." He smiled, showing a line of stone teeth. "Gargoyles use events to mark the passage of time rather than humans do with their calendar. We measure life...in different ways than humans. Your existence is so brief. Fragile."

"Gargoyles are born." I shook my head, the concept so foreign. "I'm not even going to ask how."

"We are birthed of stone. With love, comes life. If a gargoyle ceases to love—himself, others—to stone will he return."

"So you're in love with yourself," I quipped, straightening damp skirts as the feeling began to return to my limbs.

"I love," he replied simply.

I regretted my joke, outclassed beside this ancient being. "I'm sorry," I murmured. The sky brightened a little more, the world I knew beginning to wake. Dolion stirred beside me, climbing with tortured movements to his pedestal. "Do you die—" I caught myself again and wished I hadn't spoken at all.

"I am not as Sebastian," Dolion replied slowly. "I can move through the day, but I am tired, and in rest, I become as I was until I wake. Sit by me any time, Gisella."

I nodded, rising as he settled on his pedestal, resuming his pose of before. A flicker of his eyes reminded me a being lived within the stone. I stood with him a minute more, then turned to face the dark-ened house, walking to the path that would lead back to the drive. The servants might populate the place, but without Sebastian, I would be alone again, and that tore at my heart.

It's real, I screamed within the confines of my mind,

but I couldn't sense Sebastian's presence there at all, as though he had blocked me away, locking me out. Amy's memory left me contaminated and more alone than ever. A bone-deep tiredness overtook me, and I longed for my own bed. Two steps along the path, a thought occurred to me, and I turned back, unsure if he would be able to answer me.

"You know my name?"

A minute nod from the stone man as the sun crested the horizon in a burst of gold that filled the garden with light. "Sebastian speaks of you every night."

I frowned. "But I've just arrived."

"Not in his mind."

The gargoyle closed stone lids and was still.

I trudged back to the house and pressed against the door. It opened under my touch, though I was too tired to be surprised. No one was about as I slipped into the murky hall, though the place looked spotless. I was glad, knowing I must look a sight, and made it back to my room without being accosted with questions and concerns.

There I undressed silently, slipping beneath the covers to find a hot brick at the end of the bed. Had Minette watched me return to the gardens? God alone knew what she and the others thought.

I pressed numb toes to the stone's wrappings but fell asleep before feeling returned to them, my dreams haunted by stone men and men of flesh with stone in their hearts.

CHAPTER FOURTEEN

SEBASTIAN

Her feelings for me weren't real and mine...were.

The dichotomy of the betrayal, of never being rid of the sorceress who implanted herself inside my head centuries ago and refused to leave brought me to the bitter edge of my sanity.

And so I stood at the furthest reach of the property I had purchased for myself beside a man birthed of stone who fished in a swamp and liked to make meals from the prehistoric lizards the overpopulated the waters.

A final salute of one predator to another.

Why not? Because otherwise I would scream myself senseless into the void until nothing remained. And yet, I couldn't let go of the tang of defeat, and hated myself all the more for it.

What was one more dose in a daily regime four hundred years in the making?

"You mope loudly, my friend," Dolion murmured, dangling his line as the dusk turned to full night and light lit a few of the swamp houses buried deep within the bayou's depths. "Loud enough to damage my chances of a meal."

"You should eat something real, for a change." I turned my back to him, and the river. Perhaps one of his pet alligators would take a leg off and leave me to bleed out for an eternity stuffed beneath a log. The ignominious end I deserved.

"And boring," Dolion commented. "She hasn't left you yet."

"Because you are the perfect courtesan," I snapped, turning back to face him in full. "I love? What the fuck sort of wizardry do you call that?"

My gargoyle snapped his line and leaned his head back, letting one leg dangle in the water, his flesh changing to stone on command.

I envied him the control over his nature, the display more than anything I currently had.

"It is a simple truth. I love, or I don't exist at all. You know how a stone birth works," he said, his tone tinged with impatience for the first time. "This is not a conversation we need to have again, my friend."

Regret swamped me. "You're right. It's not."

Dolion's attempt to turn entirely to stone on me halted mid-progress. "Did you just apologize to me, Sebastian?"

I offered him the ghost of a smile, a little of my earlier pain easing. "The damage she's already done to me."

My smile was returned. "To us both."

His line jiggled. I shifted back, knowing he wanted no interruption to his nightly fun, but kept an eye on him, lest the evening didn't quite go the way he expected.

A single bubble marred the surface around his line, and less than a breath later the water exploded around his stone form as the alligator launched itself at the man it saw sitting on the riverbank.

What it didn't expect was the blade in Dolion's stone fist to gut it, neck to groin along its pale flesh as it rose from the water, nor the man's plaintive voice as he curled thick arms around its ridged back, while its life force spilled on the earth where he had sat a moment before.

"A little help? This will feed the servants for a full week."

"More, if they ration as they should."

"It's not like you are short of a penny."

"Still counting in a coin you were never born to, I see."

Our banter continued as I helped Dolion drag the beast from the waters, glistening intestines trailing its demise. His deft hands made short work of the meat while I skinned the behemoth in a single pull.

"Do you want me to save you anything?" Dolion

eyed the night's catch with a professional gaze, albeit a hungry one.

My gut clenched on nothingness. "This sort of fare doesn't appeal to me."

His yellow eyes rose to meet mine. "Ah. But there is a sort that will, back in the house," he murmured.

"Perhaps." I shrugged off the need to sprint back to see her, wrap my body around hers.

Not that she'd crave me the way she should. Or rather that she would, but her feelings weren't her own. My chest bore down on an empty cavity at the thought of holding her, kissing her sweet lips turned up to mine, the way she let me take from her...all false.

She'd be up soon, if I knew her adjusted nightly routine. Seeking me, but I wouldn't be there tonight. And she needed to learn that, too. I had...other work. "I need to see her." I nodded in the direction of the lights beyond the rippling waters, and the remains of the impressive carcass.

Dolion snorted. "As you will. Make sure I get a belt, this time."

I smiled and wrapped the skin into a bundled, hefting it beneath my arm as I pushed through the under growth away from the house.

Dolion's voice gave me pause.

"What do I say if she asks after you?"

I mulled it over for a few steps. "Tell her she is her own person." I turned back, a pathetic excuse on my lips, but Dolion was already gone. My lips turned up.

He'd tell her whatever story he saw fit, something sappy and as equally pathetic as *I love*, no doubt.

She seemed to like that.

Maybe I should try it.

I pushed through the undergrowth that dominated the path until I reached the jetty and placed my bundle into the small boat, and reached for the pole, wary of the bayou's underwater occupants.

Dolion might like to wrestle with the beasts, but I had other business tonight with a swamp witch who might have the answers I needed about my wife.

I stared into the watery eyes of the wisest creature I'd ever met with the knowledge she could end me in an instant.

Not so much this particular hedge witch who moved to the bayous; rather, her wolf-man companions, loyal to a fault who might like to bathe on rare occasion. Hell, at the rate my senses were assaulted by their lack of personal hygiene, I was ready to keel and be shunted into the next available coffin before sunrise.

"Her future is not set," the bayou witch purred, her voice rippling the waters around us where we sat on a thick buttress root, a small, hand crafted table made of the same tree between us.

A python slithered from beneath the many shawls twisted around her skeletal frame, but in my not so limited experience, the relocated witch was not as fragile as she appeared.

One of her many talents in shifting her shape,

along with the wolfmen who protected her between sunrise and sunset when the other predators came out to play. Another of her serpentine friends coiled around my ankle and nested there.

I ignored it.

"And mine, with her?" I asked, terse.

"Manners, Sebastian. Or have the years eroded those as well as your sense of survival?" She stared at me through brittle silver lashes, shuffling her tarot cards.

One drifted from the middle of the deck to the jetty planks beneath my feet, face down. I reach for it. "Apparently not," I murmured.

Her sandaled foot slapped my fingers away, and the snake nestling around my ankle collected the thing for her like a trained pup.

"*Never* touch the cards," she hissed, her voice echoing weirdly as I withdrew my hand.

"My apologies." I watched from my retreated place, pretending to ignore the hairy behemoth at my back and wishing I hadn't come to this deity forsaken place.

Or maybe there were too many deities residing within these tepid waters lapping at the swamp witch's doorstep, crowding mortals away.

My mortal.

The memory of Gisella in my arms, her pale throat exposed as she screamed for me last night, rose unbidden. My breeches tightened, and the wolfman behind me growled his disgust at my arousal for a woman who was safely miles away.

Thank a god who no longer acknowledges me.

A battle my soul, the remaining fragment I clutched to, childlike in my desperation for forgiveness of a sin that wasn't mine to beg penance of in the first place, I continued daily with no answer.

Until Gella arrived, and my chance at a clean slate offered me a sliver of hope for the first time in half a millennium.

Until the bayou witch flipped the card over and smiled.

"The five of cups," she whispered, drawing out the last sounds to wrap around us, weaving her magic. I flicked my chin, but her voice locked me in place as I listened beyond what she said and *felt*. "Loss. Regret. So much taken from you, Sebastian. And it will flow over your cup into hers." Her eyes snapped back to mine as she swiveled the card to face me, upside down. "But the card is reversed. Luck may be with you both. What you see as irreparable, she views as a hurdle to drag you across. Oh, it will hurt. Ache and tear. And you will forgive her everything she does. Almost everything," she added, flicking the card on the table.

I blinked, and the card depicting the five of cups disappeared beneath her shawls, along with her scaly friend.

"Fascinating," I murmured, shaking my shoulder free of the clawed paw that gripped me, still featuring an opposable thumb.

I flicked the monster's digit and he backed off, shaking his hand, the fur retreating into his skin.

Who harbors the devil within here?

"It's almost daylight, nightwalker," the swamp witch muttered. "Best be back to your cave before death takes you."

"Thank you." I flicked an emerald from my family's collection onto the table as payment for her tortures. "I'll be back."

Not that I wanted to return to her, but this place called to me, to us all, and she damn well knew it. None of us could stay away from her readings, desperate to know our pasts wouldn't collide and destroy the futures of those we loved.

Or that we would earn love in some future version of our twisted selves.

As I climbed aboard the small punt and made my way back through the convoluted river system to where Dolion waited, sans river monster, the skin draped over his shoulders like a cloak, his words echoed through my mind.

I love.

A simple but powerful statement, and a fool's errand.

But we all wore that facade here.

CHAPTER FIFTEEN

GISELLA

Stars decorated the sky when I awoke, clammy and cold. A breeze fluttered a hot wind against my naked skin. I closed my eyes, hoping to return to the nothingness of slumber, but sleep evaded me. After tossing for some time, my stomach convinced me to rise on my new schedule.

I dressed carelessly in a gown that had been laid out—Minette was running my life for now—rolled my hair into a bun and pinned it to the crown of my head. Fresh slippers were lined in neat rows by the door. The ones I destroyed the night before were nowhere in sight.

Averting my eyes from Sebastian's room, situated across the hall from mine, I peered out of my door. Every inch of me craved him. Yesterday, I would have sought him out, regardless of the time of day, or if I would encounter him in his still state. Today, that option had been removed from me. I don't know if he had even come home after the events of last night and somehow, the thought that I had evicted him from his own home made me feel worse.

Amy, what have you done to me?

My mind screamed the question into nothingness as I slipped a calm, brittle facade over my emotions, walking down the stairs at a sedate gait to find anyone at all.

I didn't have to search for Charleton, though I knew the hour was late—this household didn't run the usual hours and was too far from anywhere for anyone to care. He greeted me at the entrance to the dining room.

"Madame." He dipped his head a little, a sign of respect I hadn't earned. "I will have dinner made up for you." He gestured to someone out of sight, and turned back to me, a half-smile on his face.

"Is he—" I stepped through the doorway, halting in the empty room.

Charleton frowned. "I believe the master is away, madame. Would you like to dine in the library, perhaps?"

I nodded, turning to conceal the tears that sprang to my eyes, and made my way back to the small library, refusing the memories of my last encounter with Sebastian in this room that sprang to the forefront of my mind.

I ate alone that night, and the night after.

By the third day after our argument, I managed to wake myself soon after dawn. My internal clock had been thrown out of sync by the alternating days and nights spent with my husband, but I missed the sunlight. Needing to do more than eat, and return to my bed, I sought some other form of occupation.

Minette flustered around me, but I waved her down.

"I'm glad to have any company at all," I smiled. She dipped into a quick curtsey. "The estate—what other functions does it have?"

Minette stared at me in surprise. "None, madame."

"None?"

She shook her head, curls bobbing around her heart-shaped face. "The estate provides...distance to the master, is all."

"He uses it to hide here? No rents, no livestock? Plantation?"

"None."

I raised my eyebrows. He let a place like this run into the ground because he was afraid of the people? "Well, I'm sure there can be some function that might be derived from the land."

Alarm flared in her eyes. "He might not like that, ma'am."

"He might not like a few things. Are there any neighbors?"

She shook her head, eyes widening. "The bayou community?"

I frowned. "Who are they?"

"Granny Smythe leads them. No one can visit."

"No one?"

"No, madame." She spun on the spot, collecting my nightclothes. "It is forbidden. There are...animals there."

I smiled humorlessly. "More frightening than Sebastian?"

"Oh, much." She looked at me, then seemed to realize what she'd said. "Madame, forgive me. I am so sorry—"

"Minette. If you don't start using my name, I'll start doing my hair on my own." I threw the threat out in a gentle tone but fixed her with a sharp eye, though we both knew I was joking. The corners of her mouth turned up as she bobbed another curtsey. "And stop doing that."

The poor maid stood stock still. I laughed, unable to help the breach in etiquette, but I didn't care. She gave me a rueful smile, heading for the door, laundry collected in her thin arms.

Smiling to myself, I collected a book I'd been reading, ready to spend some time in the gardens, determined not to be afraid of the maze.

"Minette," I called, halting the maid at the door. "Would you locate a small basket of food for me to take outside?"

The bemused maid bopped a half curtsey, turned bright red, and exited in a flurry of nightclothes.

"Could you chew any louder?"

"Would you like me to try?" I swiveled around to face Dolion. He gave me a slow grimace. "Does it hurt to move when you're like this?" I gestured to his stone form. "Do your legs get tired, crouching there?"

"Does your mouth cease their insidious questions?" he groaned. "We've kept my existence secret for over a decade, and in the space of a week, you've risked that effort on a multitude of occasions."

"Are you telling me you dislike my company?"

Dolion grinned. "Not at all. Expose away." He yawned. "It's a boring way to pass the time. Especially with no events to mark my passage."

"You're obsessed with time," I pointed out, scattering crumbs on the surface of the water pooling around him. Ducks pecked at them, edging closer to me. I dropped the remainder of the roll at their feet. Feathers fluttered in the water, showering me in a spray of droplets as they attacked the bread in a flurry.

Dolion stopped pouring water when I arrived, and was happier to talk than bide his daylight hours in solitude. I hadn't asked how the fountain function worked and didn't ever intend to investigate his anatomy.

"You would be, too, if you watched days go by as a garden fixture." He snorted derisively. Water splattered water, frightening the ducks. I grimaced. "You're turning my fountain feral, *petite lynx*."

Better than Sebastian's preferred 'little hellion'.

"I bet you say that to all the girls." I fluttered my eyelashes at him. His bellowing laugh filled the garden, frightening the ducks, who sprinkled me with fountain water in their distress. "Dolion...I have a favor to ask."

"That sentence has never meant good things." He crouched back on his haunches.

I took a breath. "I want you to take me to see Granny Smythe."

Stone eyebrows rose so high, I thought they might crawl over his bald dome. "Why do you want to see Granny Smythe?"

"So you'll take me to see her?"

"Not yet."

I waited. The eyebrow arched again, and I gave in. "She might know something about Amy."

"Amy. Oh, *petite lynx*, do not go down that path."

I chewed my lip, looking down at my hands. "It's all right."

"But you'll go without me, won't you? And who will take you?"

"Minette has been there. I think."

"You endanger your maid in this."

I nodded. "Yes. It's selfish. I'm sorry. But I need answers, for both of us." I made small fists with my hands and stood. "Thank you for listening. You won't tell him?"

Dolion's head cocked to the side. "He is but a fool for avoiding you in this. I will take you. Tomorrow."

My heart leapt. "You will? Thank you—"

"On one provision."

"That sentence never precedes anything good," I smiled as I tossed his words back at him, lessening their sting, but the gargoyle maintained his grotesque appearance.

"We tell him." Dolion's expression remained fierce as I opened my mouth to object, but he held up a hand. "Afterwards."

I closed my mouth. "Well, better to beg forgiveness than ask permission."

"I'll meet you at the jetty before the sun rises. Please warn your maid of me. Screaming sets some mineral inside me reverberating. It is most disconcerting."

"It's freezing. What does he look like?" Minette held aside half a weeping tree for me to pass. "That path." She indicated a swamp ash laden fork to our right.

The jetty was set back quite a way from the house. We walked for an hour, and I began to understand how large the estate was.

"He'll be stone, I think, when you see him."

"How does he move? How does he eat?" Far from being afraid, Minette was inquisitive about the stone man.

Perhaps it came from being a maid in a vampyre's household. Her questions continued the entire journey. I began to understand how Dolion must feel as I threw query after query his way and promised myself I wouldn't beleaguer him with questions again.

"I'm not sure how his body works." I stepped over a slippery patch on the path and grabbed her hand to help her across.

"You didn't ask?"

"I...didn't want to know." I blinked at the admission.

Sebastian's words ran around my head as if he was still speaking to me, though I hadn't heard nor seen him since the night I'd been lost in the maze and met Dolion. Unease grew in my stomach.

If I had the answers to give him, perhaps he would return to me? Dolion saw him, spoke to him. Surely, he would listen to his friend. I stepped around a moss-covered rock, halting as undergrowth around us on both sides waved in the non-existent air. *This was a mistake.* I turned to see both sides of the pathway, gripping Minette's hand tightly.

"I shouldn't have brought you," I whispered.

"I wanted to be here, madame."

A crack to my right turned both our heads. Shadows swayed in the pre-dawn light, dark and featureless. One broke away from the rest, shifting closer.

I swallowed, then peered forward. "Dolion?"

His face broke into a grin, and I launched myself forward, wrapping my arms around his shoulders. "Who else?"

"Cheeky bastard," I threw the half compliment at

him, then remembered too late I'd learned it from Amy.

Drawing back, I noted his skin was soft, despite still appearing like stone. His hands tightened around mine.

"Should you not introduce us?" His gaze fixed behind me.

I stepped back. "Of course. Minette, Dolion. He is —" I stopped, flustered.

"*Une souris*." He bowed.

Minette stared. "Monsieur," she whispered, bobbing, never taking her eyes from him.

I looked between the two of them, but it was as if I wasn't there, at all. I sent a quick apology toward the house at James, knowing that after this moment, his courtship with Minette may as we never have existed at all. After a moment I coughed and stepped back— right into the water.

Sinking to my knees with a cry, I flapped, swiveling around for anything to grasp. My knees encased in mud, I couldn't move them, but continued to sink at an alarming rate. Spotting the jetty, I launched towards it, flailing.

My fingertips hit jagged edges of old wood but failed to grip anything substantial. The water closed around my chest when large hands grabbed both my arms and yanked me unceremoniously from the sludge with a disgusting slurping sound.

Mud puddled around me as Dolion deposited me on the jetty.

"Tuck your legs away," he advised, staring into the swirling sludge.

I slipped my mud-clad feet beneath me, peering into the churning water. A pair of eyes rose from the swirling mess, then another. I stared, knowing what I was seeing but unable to look away.

"Are those—"

"Yes," Dolion helped Minette into the boat, murmuring something to her in French that I couldn't hear.

He held out his hand to me as I rose gingerly, my mud-laden skirts sticking to my legs. Sigh, I hoisted them around my knees, stepping down into the small boat, conscious of the many eyes on us.

"This is safe?" I heard the doubt in my own voice.

Dolion jumped into the boat, rocking it. Water sloshed either side of the too-small craft, and I began to doubt my own sanity at the request to take us where I knew Sebastian would object.

Something beneath the waterline bumped the side of the boat. Minette squeaked, wrapping her arms around my waist and burying her head against my back. My gaze narrowed as Dolion withdrew a long pole encrusted with mud at one end from the side of the jetty.

I glared at the stone man. "That wasn't necessary."

"Fun, though."

"Indeed."

Silence fell as he lifted the pole. We skimmed across the surface for a time in silence, until light began to filter through the overhanging foliage, a golden glow lancing through long strands of moss that dangled over the water.

The bayou waters stilled around us; a mask of serenity cast over the many eyes that observed our passing.

CHAPTER SIXTEEN

GISELLA

Dolion's skin changed with the sun's birth, the stone-like roughness disappearing into his usual, deep golden hues. Minette peered over my shoulder. I was glad he had added pants to his usual attire of nothing-ness, though I suspected clothes were optional for him.

Occasionally we passed a small, rough hut, situated back into the knot of trees and leaves, propped up on tall, roughhewn stilts as though it had grown there, not been built by human hands. No other boats or people were visible, and for all appearances, we were alone.

Dolion drew us into a short jetty, lifting Minette onto the planking in one hand. The structure looked older than the one at Sebastian's estate, if such a thing were possible. He turned to me and put a knee out.

"Gisella. We may be friends, but I won't wear mud for you."

"Understandable." I took his hand and launched with one boot from his knee to the jetty, landing with both feet on the solid surface.

Surprised I hadn't tumbled through a rotten board, I exited the tenuous platform with haste, glad to have my feet on real ground. The forced memory of my time on the ship with Amy that Sebastian had brought back in the swamp witch's house consumed me until a howl nearby halted my progress.

Minette bumped into me, clutching my sodden dress. Dolion passed us, lifting my maid around me. I raised an eyebrow which he ignored, setting her down between us. I noted how covered in mud she was, and hoped I could buy some fabric to replace her ruined dress.

Dolion tipped his head back and howled. Minette squeaked again, backing into me. I gripped her hand again as a cacophony of answering howls rose around us in a disjointed symphony Dolion alone seemed to understand.

"Is this usual?" I whispered in her ear.

She shook her head, curls trembling frantically.

Dolion grinned over his shoulder at us. "The wolves welcome you. You're not their usual taste, but..." He ran his eyes over both of us, laughter lighting his golden gaze.

I grimaced back, pushing Minette to follow him as he took to the path with his long stride. Trodden earth became a planked walkway over the water. Minette and I pattered over the boards, eager to reach land again.

Mossy branches hung around us, brushing our hair in a tunnel of green that concealed the treetop walkway from sight. Beneath the foliage, the bright light dimmed to an emerald hued twilight. Tiny, flickering lights glowed in the depths of the bayou ahead of Dolion.

He held aside dangling vines. A thin green snake hissed at me from one, its tail coiling around his arm. He caught its head between two fingers, eyeing the slithery beast, and nodded at us. "She is safe. I'll wait for you here."

I frowned at his words and opened my mouth to ask, but he jerked his head toward the lights. *All right, Dolion. But you could have said we would do this part alone.* No reply came, and I assumed he didn't have the same method of communication that I shared with Sebastian.

Had shared with him, because in the last days since Amy intruded on our life together, I had heard nothing from him. Taking a long breath of still, bayou air, I peered into the wavering light, where a house became visible the longer I looked.

Minette poked my ribs, shifting me forward while I stood lost in thought. I clattered my way up the boards until I came to a small set of stairs leading down into the house. Made of several, uneven levels, it was like something out of a fairy story—one from Charles Perrault, perhaps. Thick branches supported wood planked walls and layered roofing that spread out across the walkway as though the house had multiple entry ways.

At the base of the steps stood two huge men, both sporting long hair, and open, bedraggled shirts. Each man was musclebound, their strength evidence even beneath their meager clothing. One cupped his hands to his mouth and howled into the depths of the swamp. After a moment, a distant howl echoed back, and he turned to face me, satisfied.

It was all too easy to believe such a man could transform into the beast he mimicked. The entire scene has a whimsical feel to it, like I might step into a fairy realm and never emerge. He gestured me to the steps, his gaze tracking over my body, his lip curling at my mud-stained dress.

Ignoring his attention, I ascended with as much grace as I could, stopping at the second step to be of a height with them. Swallowing back fear, I tried to smile. "I'm here to see—"

Hands removed me from the step, placing me on the soft ground. "In there."

I nodded, squeezing my nails into my hands. The hands lingered at my waist for a moment, then dropped away. I held my breath, but the lone man's touch held none of the power of Sebastian's connection to my body. My heart panged at the loss of him over the past few days. Determined to fix whatever I could before I lost him forever, I strode into the house, my steps too loud on the board, and paused over the threshold.

Shadows filled the cluttered house. Jars and statues covered shelves adjoined to the walls. Uneven wooden furniture and a collection of silks in an array of colors looked out of place in the rustic building. Rickety stairs led to both upper and lower levels, though the staircase centered around a giant trunk that created a center point thought the entire house with its multiple stories.

"It's like something out of a dream. A fantasy," Minette whispered, still gripping my hand.

I nodded, wandering further into the house. "Hello?" I called, hoping I wouldn't bring the place down on us.

Minette began to climb the stairs, but I continued around the ancient tree to find its twin tucked away at the back of the room. Its trunk was scarred with carvings of people and places. *Events.* I smiled; Dolion would like the way Granny Smythe recorded history.

On the other side of the second tree stood a tatty armchair, covered in cushions and shawls. It took me a moment to discern the person seated amongst it all. Wispy and frail, she gave me a gummy smile, peering at me from rheumy eyes.

"Granny Smythe?" I squatted before her, mud crackling as I shifted, large, brown flakes drifting from my skirts to the floor. "My name is—"

"It's not her. And don't ever give them your name."

I jumped, pivoting on my heel to face the voice I

knew well. He stepped forward out of the shadows, bracing both arms above his head against a heavy wooden strut. His dark eyes hooded as he stared at me, a flicker of—something—lighting a familiar flame there.

I cleared my throat. "This is where you've been hiding?"

"Yes." My husband surveyed me with a curious eye. "What in all the hells happened to you?"

"She fell in the bog." Dolion appeared around the tree trunk, towing Minette along with him. The small maid appeared pale and tiny beside his bulk. I noted his hands on her waist with a wry smile. She appeared to have forgotten about poor James as predicted, back at the estate. "I dragged her out again."

"You should have left her there." Sebastian glared at his friend. "We'll have words later."

Dolion rolled his eyes. "Pup."

I stared between the two men and realized with a start that Dolion had a good century or more on my husband. He turned a sharp eye my way and winked. I grinned at the gargoyle, shaking my head at his audacity.

"You. We're leaving." Sebastian snared my arm, towing me toward a darkened hallway.

"Like hell," I snapped, yanking my arm free. "I came here to get the answers you should have given me. I wouldn't have to be here if you'd talk to me." That last came out like a plea, begging. I hated the sound and wished I could take the words back, mangle them into something else and spit them back out again.

"That's never going to happen, dearie." A woman with silver-streaked dark hair stepped between us, proffering a tray of small glasses filled with a lime-colored liquid.

Dolion bowed, while Sebastian glared at me over her head.

"Granny." Dolion rose, liberating the tray.

She hugged his waist, taking Minette by the hand and leading her away from our small crowd. I found a glass pressed into my hand. Golden eyes assessed me, but nothing happened, and I seemed to have passed his test. I smiled my thanks to Dolion, but the drink was whisked away and placed back on the tray.

"We're going," Sebastian growled, low enough to make the air around me tremble.

I held his gaze, though fear plagued me—not of him, but whether I'd made a huge error coming here without trying harder to speak to him first. While I fought my indecision, the glass was placed back into my hand.

I nodded to Dolion, who watched his friend with a frown, and tossed the liquor back before Sebastian could take it away. Sebastian's hand tightened on my arm, his presence roaring into my head where it stayed silent for so long. I tugged back, but he held me in a firm grip, pulling me against him.

Where before I would have found the action arousing, intimate, all I met now was a hard, closed face void of emotion and heart.

"I've had plenty of time to think about who you really are, *Gella*."

I frowned, forgetting to pull away. "Who I am? I'm... me." His words made no sense but that didn't change whatever he thought he saw in my head. He snorted, towing me out the door. "Sebastian. Stop, I'm not—"

He turned on me with a snarl. "You'll come with me, and if you choose not to walk, I'll pick you up and hurl you back into the sludge you came from."

I froze, sensation draining from me, numbness replacing it with speed. Blinking back tears and knowing I was well out of my depth, I stopped fighting and let him drag me across the room.

"You will not take a woman by force, in this way or any other." Granny Smythe was at the doorway faster than I could follow.

"You're fast," I mumbled. Numbness crept along my arms in silent fingers, the alcohol taking fast effect on my body.

Sebastian laughed, still gripping my arm. "Get out of my way, witch."

Granny Smythe smiled and pressed a hand to his chest. Sebastian dropped to the floor with a resounding thump and began to snore.

She smiled at me. "He shouldn't speak that way to his elders."

I blinked. "How many of you ancients are there?" I managed to croak.

The crone shook her head, gesturing me across to where Minette was seated at a small table. Dolion passed me another glass, and went to attend his friend.

"Can you teach me how you did that?" I asked, aiming to have something to say, all sense of manners deserting me.

"Of course." Granny Smythe smiled at me. "Sit."

I did sit, unsure if it was by my choice or her command. So many things in the last few days slipped out of my control, though that had been the story of my life for the past year. First the king's purchase of me and the other girls away from our homes, then the ship across the seas, the abbey and finding my home with Sebastian.

I had been with him for less than a month, and already I knew my heart would shatter if he forced me to leave.

And go where?

He snored on at my feet and didn't answer. *I shouldn't have come here without understanding more of his fear.* My hands began to shake, and I hid them in my mud-encrusted skirt.

"I'm so sorry to bring all this here, to you." Tears pricked at my admission, and I peered down to hide those, too.

"This was always like to come, dear. Now, have the drink the nice stone totem gave you."

Dolion snorted across the room, shaking his head. I was glad to take that order, too, letting the liquid slide down my throat in a single gulp. Warmth spread into my limbs.

"What is that?" I rasped.

"Bayou rum. Plantations always have the best stuff. With a few little additives of my own, of course."

"Of course," I grinned, beginning to get a gauge of the crazy woman.

"Now, you want to know about Anitta."

"Amy— yes, I know her by another name."

"Many do," she said enigmatically, sliding a white bundle across the table. It was so bright I could barely look at it until she pressed a hand to the cloth. The glow diminished as if by a silent command. "I've been trialing a new silk, one that tells the prying person to *kass twa*."

Her Creole words rolled over her tongue with emphasis, but her meaning was clear. The cloth parted under her hands, revealing a handsome stack of vibrant blue cards, much larger than the average deck of playing cards. Each one was about the length of my hand with all my fingers extended.

Dolion returned, lifting Minette and placing her across his lap to slide into the chair beside me. She didn't so much as squark but curled her hands around his shoulders as though hanging on for dear life.

Granny Smythe smirked. "It's so sweet when the olds find new love."

"You know I can hear you," Dolion said from behind Minette's mop of curls.

"Yes, dear. Of course." She shuffled the cards, sending several in a straight line towards me. When five were lined in a neat row, she looked at me expectantly.

"What am I supposed to do?"

"Put your hands on the cards, of course."

"Of course," I muttered, more out of my depth than before. "Is this magic?"

"Well, we could call it voodoo to get you in the mood." She sent me an impish grin, her eyes sliding to Dolion. "I could get out my snakes and shake some rattles, but it's not in me. There are plenty it's for, but not this witch."

"Is that what you are?" My hands were drawn to the cards, dealt face down. I hovered over them, indecisive. "You know, strangers might take you more seriously if you showed some age," I muttered, trying to decide between two end cards.

"If I did that, the nice young men," she patted Dolion's bicep, and Minette slapped her hand away, "might not come calling."

"Is that what you think they do?" My hands couldn't choose and, not being the most patient person, I slapped them both down, to see what would happen.

The table rippled. Like water, the entire surface became fluid, its edges flowing in waves. Granny Smythe scooted back, her hands held high in the air. Dolion lifted Minette in his arms, tossing her away from the table to the rug in the center of the room behind us.

Everything on the table turned the blue of the deck of cards, rippling in rows of waves and eddies that shouldn't have been possible. Drawn to the movement, I leaned forward, swaying as I had on the ship. Something in the water called to me, something beneath the surface.

Impatient, I pressed closer, desperate to see what it was. Strong hands gripped my shoulders, hauling me upright. I struggled, ripping and tearing at the thick arms around me, but they refused to release me, dragging me back from the water and its siren call.

"Stay with me, Gella." His voice was rough in my ear, bringing me back, centering me. "Please." That last had an edge of desperation, and instead of me begging, it was him.

And that was enough to break the spell and bring me back.

"Sebastian," I gasped. My hands uncurled, clinging to him, rather than fighting.

"Tell me," Granny Smythe commanded, her eyes the color of the ocean.

I sank forward again, but Sebastian held me upright. A roar filled my ears, and I was back with the ship. Not on it, but seeing it from the outside, as though I were a bird flying at its side. Wind rushed against me, chilled and full of salt. I screamed as that salt was torn away, rent through my skin. The air across the watery table white. Tiny crystals formed, suspended in the air between us and the crone.

Then the waves crashed over me, and I lost myself in their chaos.

"Gella!" Sebastian yelled in my ear, but all I could see were waves and white caps, the unbroken surface. I needed to dive down, find what was beneath, to claim what called to me.

"It's taking her!"

I wrestled in his arms, twisting, yanking, but he was iron to my lace. As I came back to myself, I knew there was nothing between us but the ashes of our souls clashing, then rent apart.

His face came level with mine, his lips moving, though I didn't understand a word of whatever language he whispered. I pressed my hands to his cheeks, holding on as the water calmed around me, numbing, soothing, stilling.

Then the world returned in full force.

I stared at Granny Smythe until her eyes returned to a human form, though I doubted that anyone could convince me of who could be considered *normal* here. Exhaling a salty breath, I turned in Sebastian's arms, pressing my cheek to his shoulder, his shirt dry. Neither of us were covered in sweat, nor did I have a tear to pass for my trials.

She had taken salt from us.

"What does it mean?" I looked up at him, relying on him to give me the truth, though I knew he could withhold it if he chose.

I trust you.

The gentle brush of his consciousness against mine offered an additional layer of comfort as I burrowed deeper into the security of his broad arms.

"I don't know." He stared straight at the swamp witch, pressing me to him.

Between us, warmth began to grow.

CHAPTER SEVENTEEN

GISELLA

I clung to Sebastian's chest, the sway of the ocean leaving me. Over my head, he fired questions at the swamp witch, barely letting her answer one before he threw the next her way. Glad to have his violent rage focused anywhere else than on me, I closed my eyes, letting him take over. Throughout my order and recovery, he crushed me tight to him, steadfast.

This is the man I can rely upon.

Whatever had frightened him before was gone, though I still didn't know how, or why. My own mind had a blank space where my thoughts roamed free. I ignored that for the time being, too exhausted to fight for anything other than sleep.

Granny and Sebastian bickered over my head. I disregarded it all until he tensed around me, his volume rising to a roar that stilled everything in the vicinity.

"What did you take from her?" Sebastian shouted the words over my head. His frustration became evident as his voice cracked, a horrid sound that jarred me from my internal study.

"I took what your girlfriend put into her."

"What?" Brain function returned enough for me to comprehend that single line. I twisted in the circle of Sebastian's arms, looking over my shoulder at the ancient witch. "What do you mean?"

Granny Smythe smirked. "Didn't you know your husband had a fling with the *sorciere*? That little tryst lasted a few hundred years at last count, didn't it, dear?"

Sebastian nodded once, and that fast, my whole world crumbled.

"Why didn't you tell me?" I whispered, clutching his shirt. I wasn't sure if I wanted to cling to him or pummel him into oblivion. It didn't matter because inside my head, somewhere, I had *known*. The way Amy stood behind him in those portraits, the intimate closeness they shared, even in his most tortured, darkest hours. She was *there* with him.

I looked up to read Sebastian's face, but he didn't look down but stared out, over me.

The warmth between us died, replaced with the void I knew too well.

Don't close me off from you, please.

But he had no response to give me.

"What is the salt for?" he ground out, his hands painfully tight on my back.

"Oh, Sebastian. Isn't it obvious, even to you?" She shook her head. I watched her reflection act out her part in the stained-glass circular window behind Dolion and Minette. Her face coated in blues and greens, she took on an ethereal figure. "Amy put a barrier between you. Salt can protect, or separate. For you, it was the latter. For Gisella, it was protection. From the moment she saw you, she was sheltered from your more...charming personality traits."

"Unlike yours." Frustration rumbled through him.

"Do you hear what she is saying to you, you great oaf!" Minette, who had been uncharacteristically silent throughout the entire exchange burst out. "Gisella's love for you is real—not pretend, or fake, or created or whatever you thought! You've frightened her, bullied her, and all she has done is love you!"

The room fell silent again, the rare movement were the gazes that flicked between my husband and my maid. Minette's eyes widened to their farthest extremes, whites lining her liquid brown gaze. She clapped both hands over her mouth, her cheeks stained red as she sank back against Dolion's chest.

He wrapped thick arms about her, resting his chin on the top of her blonde curls. A wry grin crept across his face. "Well, brother. Couldn't have said it better myself."

Dolion settled back, maintaining his smarmy grin,

grabbing another drink from the tray and downing it in one.

I doubted it even touched the sides on its way down.

Can a gargoyle be intoxicated?

"I think that settles it, then." Granny Smythe packed her cards away, wrapping them once again in the white cloth, which became blindingly bright once she had taken her hands away from the material.

I squinted and hid my eyes in Sebastian's shirt.

He didn't move. "Is that all?"

"What more do you want, Sebastian?" For the first time, Granny Smythe sounded tired. "You came here, sulking. You came seeking answers." I chanced a look over my shoulder. She gestured at us. "And you leave with something more than many far greater in age than you ever achieve."

She leaned back on the hardwood chair, lines decorating her face I was sure hadn't been there moments before. I regretted my choice of words to her, before.

"Thank you." I inclined my head, as much as Sebastian's arms would allow. "We're grateful." I kicked his shin.

He gave no response. Minette giggled somewhere to my left.

"Don't be too thankful, love."

I stared upwards. "Whyever not?"

Sebastian clenched his teeth; I was getting no further response from him.

It was Dolion who answered. "Because she's waiting for payment."

"Oh." I twisted in his arms and addressed Granny Smythe. "How do we pay you?"

I was careful of my words, having grown up on stories from the Black Forest of elves and fairies who demanded debt of agreements and refused to be tricked by my ignorance of this world.

Dolion grinned over Minette's head, and relief swamped me. I was glad to have another ally in this chaotic menagerie of magical folk.

Granny Smythe smiled—a thin slash between tight lips.

"Blood."

I opened my mouth to make some snide remark, but Sebastian stopped me.

Allow me, Gella, please. We can argue later.

I was so relieved to have his voice back in my head, I didn't register his exhaustion until he was already speaking.

"Whose?"

"Hers, of course." Granny's voice washed over me. She had already taken salt, and Sebastian drank from me like I was his personal liquor cupboard. What more was a little drop? Sebastian's arms tightened around me. "Oh, my child, I wouldn't dream of taking from your wife. I want Anitta's blood."

"Are you making light of us?" I asked, confused. I swiveled back to face Sebastian, my neck tight from the rally of back and forths.

Not now, Gella.

I felt like a disobedient child, told to leave best alone or to sit in the corner for some misdeed. Even in my own home growing up, I hadn't been ignored or left out of conversations...until the one that left me homeless and another man's property.

After that trauma, I refused to think of my neediness as petty. Lack of control over my life haunted me, and I refused to let that go in silence, cowering meek and quiet while others decided my fate. No, if my life was going to tear apart, I wanted to be able to blame myself for its shortcomings, not leave it in the hand of a pair of crusty old *has-beens*.

Are you quite done?

I clenched my teeth, my toe beginning to tap. Broad hands squeezed my arms, and I was glad he recognized my impatience.

"She needs the power," Sebastian spoke slowly. "To keep herself looking like this. Us. How much?" This last came in a resigned tone.

"You agree, then?"

"Depends on the quantity," Sebastian fired back.

"More than a few drops, I assure you."

"Good. Any less wouldn't be worth my time."

"Bring what you get. I'll wait."

Sebastian nodded, gathering me to him. Powerful thighs beneath me pushed us up. Beside us, Dolion rose, lifting Minette with him. At the door to the stairs, Sebastian ushered me through without giving me a chance to farewell the odd, lonely woman in her swamp. Fireflies swarmed my head, but even in my distraction, I heard his answer to her.

"Come and claim what you like. But I won't wait for you. Her life is mine now."

Sebastian clasped one hand tightly, Minette gripping my other hand, and together Dolion led us along the walkway across to the small boat. I stepped into the small coracle, barely aware of our surroundings. The light dimmed between mossy boughs, night coming on across a darkening sky. How long had we sat in the witch's house? Like Dolion, time appeared to pass in a different measure there.

The stone man pushed us away from the wharf, small eddies whirling sludge and muck that clung to the sides of the small boat. My mind still whirled from the memories and faces jammed into my head. Well, what had been put there. Granny said she had removed her presence, but some part of me worried that my mind wasn't my own. After all, I heard voices that weren't mine on a regular basis, and answered them too.

I twisted to find my own demon standing tall above me, a pole gripped in his hands as he propelled us through the bayou waters, doubling Dolion's earlier pace. Surprised that all four of us fit in the small boat without the thing sinking, I nudged Sebastian's foot.

"How do we get her to come to us?"

"Virgin sacrifices always work." Dolion's eyes lit up, but Minette colored.

He tracked the flush rising from her modest neck-line to her cheeks, earning him a glare from both of us.

"Oh, well done," Sebastian snarked.

Dolion shrugged, still grinning, and turned back to steer the boat to the estate.

"I don't know." Sebastian freed one hand to run it over his hair. With several days' growth on his chin, he looked wilder than ever, especially next to Dolion's smooth features. I wondered if it was a gargoyle thing. "She won't come alone. Anitta is attracted to...glamorous occasions."

Don't stare too long, love.

I turned my glare on him, but it didn't last long. His shadowed jaw enhanced his aquiline beauty. I leaned against his leg, taking comfort in the solidarity of his presence. At least he was talking to me again.

"Maybe we could—" I stalled, an idea forming in my head, but I couldn't say it.

Amy seemed to have formed a link between me and Sebastian, but how to bring her out...without putting someone in harm's way? But he was right; I remembered the handsome young man in the carriage with her at the New Orleans dock and shuddered to consider his purpose in her life.

Don't even think about it, Gella.

Sebastian's warning tone put me on edge.

"Well, what would you do, then?" I snapped.

Two heads turned my way in surprise, and I remembered far too late that they hadn't been privy to our conversation.

Sebastian stilled as though turned to stone himself at the end of the boat.

You may as well be the one who freezes each night to match your day.

I regretted the spiteful idea the moment I thought it, but still, not an inch of him moved.

"Why don't you hold a ball?" Minette's voice carried across the water, and I repressed the urge to shush her.

Sebastian turned, surveying her with interest. "How would that achieve our goal?" he asked carefully, and I knew he was loath to involve such an innocent into an act of preconceived murder.

An idea I had taken to with so little resistance. Maybe we were suited, after all.

"It doesn't matter how old she is. It's still murder," I muttered.

She has done more than her fair share of bloodletting in her time.

"Yes, but I wasn't privy to that, thank God." Sebastian winced and I closed my mouth with a snap.

"If you held a masked ball, wouldn't that give her the opportunity to come into your home? Achieve— whatever she wants to do?" Minette asked.

Dolion flashed her a sharp smile while my head started to pound. Running more than one conversation at a time was exhausting.

Sebastian nodded, glancing down at me. "Yes. That might work."

Minette smiled. "You might need to get used to the company." She jabbed me with her elbow.

"Maybe," I said, watching my husband with concern as he resumed his sentry post at the back of the boat.

The light dimmed around us as dusk fell in full over the bayou. What sedate creatures that had been silent throughout the day awoke, chirps and cries echoing over the still waters. I shivered, feeling very much the prey in a land of predators.

The jetty approached quickly. I helped Minette off the boat, Dolion launching himself with apparent ease to land further along the jetty than should have been possible. He caught her elbow, helping her up, and led her along the wooden planks, her fine pale hand clasped in his darker one.

I stared after them, bemused.

But he's not human, love. And neither am I.

Left in the boat with Sebastian, I felt the moment the air charged. He stalked toward me along the short, wooden spine. His balance was perfect; the boat neither shifted nor swayed beneath his light steps as though his bulk weighed nothing at all here.

Prey to his predator.

That's all I was, in this scenario. I didn't dare back away in case I repeated my performance of this morning.

My God, was that this morning?

"Don't swear," he growled, reaching for me.

His fingertips grazed my bare arm, leaving a searing path of woken nerves in his wake.

Suppressing a shiver, I checked along the jetty, but Dolion and Minette had already disappeared behind a swaying curtain of mossy foliage. "We should—" I started, but his hands wound around me, bringing me to stand against him. Warm lips brushed mine, sweet sensation assailing me before he leaped as Dolion had, still holding me in his arms to land in the center of the jetty.

"No point changing whatever happened this morning," he gestured at my dress.

I closed my eyes, knowing I was filthy after my dip in the drink.

Yes. But let's get you clean before we get into that.

My eyes snapped open in time to find him far too close. His mouth captured mine in a deep kiss that left my legs trembling where I stood. His hands tangled in my hair as he devoured me, and I weathered the violence of his need.

You shouldn't be so cowed, Gella. I like to see the bite in you.

An image that didn't come from my mind of me astride his hips, bare breasted and crying out enveloped me. His grip tightened, pulling me closer into him as his fantasies played out in real time inside my head.

"That's not fair," I gasped. My heart pounded in my chest.

"But you like it." His fingers trailed to my skirts, his

broad palm covering my bottom to jerk me into his hard length.

"They aren't my thoughts." I slapped his arm as hard as I could, knowing it wouldn't hurt him, though my own hand would ache from the impact. The action didn't make my blush any less, but it did give me a petty sense of satisfaction when the images stopped.

Self-flagellating already?

He laughed when I shook my stinging hand, winding his arm around me and leading me back to the house.

I pondered the day's events as we walked, making sure I hadn't missed too much in my dazed state. "Why did Granny Smythe call Amy a sorceress?" I stopped.

Sebastian frowned down at me, tugging me forward. "It's getting cool, and I won't have you dying of some sickness."

"Cool is relative." I slapped at a gnat buzzing about my head. "Stop avoiding answering me."

"Demanding little thing, aren't you?" He kissed the top of my head and sighed. "It's as good a title—name —as any for her. She uses dark magic, but she comes from a dark period of history, and so it suits her."

Some echo of admiration shadowed that remark. I managed to stop myself from hitting him again. Just.

"How do we combat someone, something like her?" I whispered.

His jaw set in a hard line. "I know her quite well."

I remembered Granny Smythe had said as much, back in the heart of the bayou. Something uncomfortable wriggled in my gut, sending a wave of nausea through me. I did my best to ignore my fear. "So, this is a jilted lover's affair, then?" I said lightly.

Sebastian snorted. "It might come under something a little more than that."

Like obsession?

"Did you love her?" I asked. All levity deserted me as a thought wound its way around my heart. "Do you still?" My whisper was lost in the rustle of the bayou as evening creatures began their nighttime activities.

"I might have convinced myself of that, once. But, no. I didn't love her, and now there is room for one alone inside what was once a heart." He halted, turning me to face him. Cool fingers caught my chin, tipping my head back. "It's you, Gella."

His mouth closed over mine, his kiss soft and sweet.

It's always been you.

I sank into him, winding my arms around his neck. His scent enveloped me, drawing me deeper as I let him kiss my fears away.

Perhaps that was a mistake.

CHAPTER EIGHTEEN

GISELLA

Minette waited at the doorway where we arrived at the house, her eyes following Dolion's loping gait as he disappeared into the garden as she addressed us.

"Madame, I can draw you a bath—"

That was as far as she got before Sebastian waved her away.

"I'll take care of Gisella myself, Minette." He fixed her with a steady eye when she looked like she might object. "Take the night off. Charleton, see that she takes some time to herself. You behaved admirably today." A flush crept up my maid's cheeks, no doubt remembering her outburst toward him.

"Please, can you send up some food?" I called as Sebastian grasped my hand, towing me up the stairs and along the hall.

I didn't get to hear Charleton's reply before Sebastian led me into a room and closed the door behind us. The door closed with the soft *thunk* of a dual lock. I took two steps inside before I halted.

Blacks and grays decorated most of the surfaces, enhanced with deep blues that formed geometric frames around each fresco. A mountain scene occupied an entire wall. Small ferns and twisted, stunted trees framed the painting where it overlooked a great dip into a valley, the opposing peaks far distant. The vista was so large I felt as though I might step into it and fall off a mountain ledge to disappear into the mist below.

Where is this?"

"Japan."

"Oh. But...this isn't my room."

It isn't your room, either.

At least, not the one we woke in together.

"No, it isn't. Not in the sense you mean." His lips grazed my nape. Every hair there stood on end at the simple, teasing gesture. He laughed softly. "But it's what you wanted."

"Yes," I whispered, turning in a half-circle.

A dark-wood four-poster bed sat against one wall, netting caught up on all sides. Gold and silver circular patterns decorated a silky cover. I returned to focus on him, watching as he unbuttoned his shirt.

Sebastian let it hang open, raking a hand through his hair. Pale, ridged flesh and hard muscle displayed in the shadows beneath the ends of his shirt.

"You need a bath." He looked down, but at me, not himself. "And you're flaking all over my carpet."

"I'm so sorry," I blurted.

His gaze followed me as I attempted to retreat to the hall we'd come from. Yes, I had craved him, but this– this room, this place seemed far more intimate and imposing, as though he had thrown off the lordly mantle and given me a true glimpse of who he was beneath.

I was nowhere near ready for this.

"Gella—" He reached for me.

I backed away, finding the door with both hands at my back. "I can clean up in my own room—"

"No." He caught my wrist, drawing me back across the room to a flat section of mahogany paneled wall next to the bed. Kicking his boot into the side unceremoniously, Sebastian paused. A crease appeared, a vertical line separating the roof and floor.

He tugged it open and led me down into a lowered, tiled area with a sunken small pool that took up most of the room. The walls looked rough, as though they were hewn from solid rock. I realized with a start that we were below the castle, inside the rock strata.

Wide paving framed the water, the edges curling gently. Steaming water poured from a twisted face in the wall, not so different from Dolion's grotesque day mask. I half expected the bodiless figure to talk to me, but it remained still. Wall sconces, not as decorative as the ones in the plush halls of his home, flickered a golden light over the pool's bluish-green surface.

"It's an underground water system." Sebastian grabbed a bag of something scented like berries and threw a handful of crystals into the water. "Dolion, Charleton and I made the most of it when we built the place. My gargoyle brought rock from the ground itself, a magical experience to watch. The rest, Charleton and I carted across the continent from one end to the other to create something that looked like home." His mouth twisted. "The place of respite seemed apt in the event we needed to hide away from the world," he mused, lost in his own head and not in mine for once.

"I can understand that need," I whispered.

Even on the continent, there were horrible stories of burnings and witch hunts that traveled from Salem across oceans. The new world of the Americas had a horrific history in their fledgling years. Both my monsters were right to prepare, even be afraid.

Crimsons and blues swirled around the pouring water from the herbs he had thrown in. Sebastian pulled a handful of what looked like sand from a different pocket in the bag and tossed that in too. The water bubbled for a moment, then settled.

"What is it?" I asked, surprised to see the pool filling at a surprising rate.

"Salts. The naturally heated water has some medicinal benefits. You'll need its properties after what she —and I—have taken from you." He dipped his head in apology, and I smiled, the muscles tight with lack of use. "Do you have a headache?"

I nodded and instantly regretted it. "Yes. But I thought it was from...everything that had happened."

"Perhaps. And you haven't eaten anything." He paused, eyeing me. "The swamp shots don't count."

"No." I twitched my nose, one hand pressed to my stomach. More mud flaked over my fingers to decorate the clean tiles. I winced.

"I am...sorry, Gella."

I held his dark gaze, losing myself in them for a moment, for eternity.

I would forgive you anything.

The corner of his mouth quirked. "Would you." It wasn't quite a statement, but it wasn't a question, either.

He offered me his promise.

A shiver rioted over my skin, setting every never-ending trembling in anticipation. Pushing the feeling aside, I turned to him, clenching the material of my skirts in my hands.

"I thought you couldn't hear me. In my head," I added in the event I was being obtuse. "I thought... after she took Amy's effects away, I would be...alone."

You have never been alone, Gella.

"I hear you." His lips moved at the same time as he spoke within my mind, and I lost myself in those eyes again.

The pool filled at an alarming rate. Or maybe I'd stared at him for that long. Either way, my lapse wasn't socially acceptable.

There's only us here, Gella.

Sebastian pressed the top of the spout. The stone face shuddered as a section of stone closed over its mouth, cutting off the flow of water. He crossed back to me, hands on my shoulders, flicking under the collar of my dress.

"Turn around, Gella." A glint in his eye told me not to argue with him.

I pivoted on my heel, telling myself I obeyed him because I wanted to be clean.

Such pretty lies you tell yourself.

He worked deft fingers on the tiny buttons that lined the back of my dress. Minette had fastened me into the garment an hour before the sun had risen. His breath hit the back of my neck. I clutched the material to my chest as he peeled the dress from my shoulders, hands sliding along my waist and tugging until I relinquished my hold and was left bare before him.

"Get in," he growled against my ear.

Gripping his hand, I stepped out of my mud-puddled dress, ignoring the flakes that detached from my legs, and slid into the water.

Warmth soaked into me as I sank into the water up to my neck. The level rose when Sebastian slipped into the pool behind me. He stood without touching me for a moment, the warmth of the waters sinking bone deep. I sighed and tilted my head back, relishing the tension that soaked in whatever he had added to the bath. His fingers ran through my hair, removing pins with the same deft attention as he'd used to remove my dress.

I shivered at the thought of him so near me as my hair tumbled to my shoulders, curling in ringlets as they touched the water's surface. One arm slipped around my waist, his feet tapping mine in an effort to make me raise my legs. Gripping his forearm tight, I gave my balance and security over to him as he drew my head back into the water.

Warmth suffused my scalp as I floated, trusting him with my safety. He rubbed his fingers in small circles, releasing stresses I hadn't known I was carrying. Was this place where he came to hide from the daylight, to sleep? Without him, it was naught but a watery, stone tomb.

I paused, his lonely existence so clear. He had traveled with a select few to remove himself from Amy, and yet, here she was, haunting us both. His companions— a servant and a friend by nature of their shared horrors, I suspected—moving with him away from all they knew.

Like me, they were orphans in an unknown land. They'd only been here a while longer.

I reached back to place a hand against his cold cheek, an ache seeping into my skin. "Just because you think you are dead does not mean you may forget to live." I smiled, rare in these days. "We will hold the ball here."

"We will?" His eyes surveyed me with amusement, a flickering storm brewing behind them.

"We will," I said firmly, "and you will see there is nothing to be feared from whom you draw apart from."

We will see about that, Gella.

He slipped around me tiny eddies, announcing his presence in the flickering light, pulling my languid body flush against him. Breath left my lips at having him so close, overloading my senses in a broken fashion. While my body knew I was pressed against him, my eyes sought the lie of the void that was his presence, cool even in the heat of the waters.

Sebastian dipped his head, his lips pressing against mine, his tongue seeking entrance. Every touch was lined with a sense of urgent need.

I could have lost you forever. To her, to my brutish lack of civility when you ran scared.

His hand cupped my head, deepening the kiss as I let him in, removing my ability to answer him, even inside my own mind. Our bodies tangled together, slick and easy, fitting one to the other as though opposing puzzle pieces. His tongue swirled against mine, bringing forth a vivid, obscene vision of his head between my legs slamming into me.

I moaned into his mouth, gushing hot against where his hard length nudged between my legs in my sensitive places.

Do you want me to do that?

Sebastian's voice echoed mockingly in my head. He tugged my hair, drawing my chin back, his teeth grazing the place he'd taken from me before earning him a shiver of appreciation. He laughed against my throat, seeking to tease every inch of my flesh above the waterline.

Sebastian's head disappeared beneath the surface, his mouth trailing kisses along my ribs and stomach. As his hands parted my knees, I gasped, the kisses turning to licks along my inner thighs. My mind caught up with his intent, a momentary war ensuing between my practical mind and my desire.

I gripped his arms, not caring if my nails bit into his skin, urging him up. He broke the surface, a quizzical look on his face.

"You can't do that," I spluttered, my face heating in a way that had nothing to do with the temperature of the water. His fingers stroked the places his mouth had been while I tried for a slice of logic that evaded me. "You'll drown!"

His smile was sinful and sad at the same time. "I don't need to breathe, Gella."

"Oh." My suspicion I hadn't had time to ask about confirmed, I released my death grip that wasn't stopping him anyway.

He slid along my body again, the water closing over his slicked hair.

This time his kisses were tiny nips, playful and light, sending a shimmer of sensation over me. When he reached my stomach, his tongue made a path downward, finding the tender flesh between my thighs.

Close your eyes. Feel everything.

My head tilted back, I let him hold me up, floating in an abyss of pleasure. Water swirled against the quick movement of his tongue and lips, entering my intimate places. Broad hands curled around the backs of my legs, holding me in place against his clever mouth. My moans echoed around the chamber, my own voice coming back to mock me, indecently wanton.

His teeth grazed my flesh, a sharp sting that drew a yelp from my lips, every nerve ending screaming, then his tongue pressed against the spot, numbing. A thin trickle of pink swirled around me, the flow cut off as his mouth fixed around the bite. His lips drawing from me brought a wave of pleasure crashing over me, until I could see and hear nothing, but feel what he did to my body like a distant observer.

He broke the surface, grasping me in relentless hands as he hauled me into his chest. His mouth found mine too fast, his kisses violent and bruising, his tongue dominating. I couldn't keep up with the speed of his movements, lost in a knot of motion as he roamed over me, around me. His hands slid over my rump, drawing me back, the tip of his cock pressing against my folds.

I grasped at the rough stone lip of the pool, the hardness beneath my hands mirroring the over-whelming strength of him as he slid inside me. I clung to the edge, willing myself to stay with him but when I stared into the void of his eyes I sank, and his arms kept me from drowning.

His fathomless gaze held me captive as he impaled me on his steel length. When he smiled, a harsh, twisted thing that left me moaning around him, sharp points extended past his garnet-stained lips. His thrusts inside me matched his earlier kisses, deep and ruining. I arched in his grasp, my screams slamming back at me until all I could hear was the pleasure that tore through me at his touch.

One hand wound around my body, sliding along my spine to caress the curve of my buttocks. His fingers slipped lower after a moment, and he stilled within me.

I opened my eyes, confused until he pressed his thick fingertip to my back entrance, pushing and testing. My breath caught, and I shook my head. "No—"

Shhh, Gella. Let me explore you.

I swallowed back a sob as he pushed his finger inside me, the tip stretching my hole. Pleasure and pain swamped my awareness as he retreated and pushed, retreated and pushed, working his way in a little deeper with every press forward. I could barely breathe as he filled me in both ways. My body trembled between his cock and his finger where he played with me. I gripped his shoulders as he pressed his knuckles to my cheeks and stilled, letting me get used to the dual sensation.

Then he thrust up into me with both finger and cock.

I screamed, my body clamping down as I took pleasure from his invasion without the assistance of his bite.

His eyes lit with dark triumph, Sebastian held me still a moment longer then took over. His hips jerked into me, hand and cock working faster, claiming every part of my body.

By every sin you feel too good, Gella.

Sebastian ripped at me, his body pounding against my flesh as the water boiled around us. His roar filled the cavern as he took his own pleasure and emptied himself inside me. I clung to him, sobbing his name until the waters ceased roiling, and my heart slowed. Then he cupped my head in his hand, tilting me so I could stare up at him.

Nothing was said between us as he lowered his mouth to my throat.

When I opened my eyes, the stilled waters around us reflected pink beneath the flickering wall sconces.

Sebastian drew my head from the water with care. I sighed my protest, but he returned with a bottle of oil he rubbed into my hair, massaging his fingers deep into my scalp. I rested back against him, my shoulders sinking beneath the water once more. His eyes glowed with dark flame as they did each time he took from me. He offered sweet kisses against my tender lips as he worked, maintaining contact between us, always.

I allowed myself to enjoy the sensations that washed over me, letting him help me to forget for a time. Thick arms circled my waist, my head resting on his shoulder with no fear of dropping beneath the surface if I slept. I floated back against him, closing my eyes as I settled into his stolen warmth and let myself forget the stresses of our unusual day.

Once we left the sunken chamber, I would have a ball to plan and how to murder a sorceress. For now, I took the refuge my husband offered and cherished every moment before our world turned to hell.

CHAPTER NINETEEN

SEBASTIAN

"Perhaps if you are gentler with her, she'll be nicer during the daylight hours."

I blinked as Charleton straightened my cravat and stare down at the bald patch on the top of his head. "I beg your pardon?"

He looked up at me, his face guileless as a newborn babe's. "Nothing, my lord."

I snarled, wrapping my hand around his throat as I pressed his back to the wall across the room in less than the time it took my valet to fill his mortal lungs.

"Say that again."

Charleton looked down at me, his slippered feet dangling a good foot above the plush bedroom carpet, and shook his head. "No thank you, my lord," he said, politely.

"Damn servants can't even be threatened," I snapped, letting him down.

Charleton straightened his jacket and returned to his duties of fluffing my cravat, albeit across the room from where he started. "It's a time of stress, sir. We all feel it."

Her most of all.

I didn't need to delve into his mind to hear the thought that rolled around my room.

"Thank you, Charleton. For all you do for us both. Is she...struggling?" I hesitated, needing to ask more, but unsure how much to give away of what I feared for Gella.

Charleton worked in silence, flicking invisible pieces of lint from my collar. "She manages, my lord. As any wife in her situation does."

"That's not an answer." *There are no others like hers.*

Our surface conversation floundered as he looked up and held my gaze in full for acknowledging the impossibility of the situation.

"Gisella lacks...love. She has no family to rely and calls servants her friends." He held up a hand. "I know our household is unique. Your situation dictates it so. But she is not from your world, and is still new to it. Who does she turn to without you? A stone man while you converse in her head, and take her sleeping hours?"

"I love her when I am able," I growled.

Charleton dropped his hands as I stalked away. "Physical contact is no substitute for a full heart, my lord." His sadness draped me, but by the time I turned back, an apology ready on my lips, he has turned away, collecting my nightclothes from the floor.

I strode along the hall, ready to find Gella and undo all the fine work Charleton just fixed.

∾

"You're worried she won't come." Dolion watched the young catfish circle the base of his fountain.

Gella had Charleton catch from the wriggling, precocious creatures at the jetty while I waited for the sun to see and see if my butler and valet still had all his limbs. The man survived, just, avoiding death and the snapping jaws of the reptilian brethren within the tepid bayou waters and filled the water feature with plenty of the juvenile fish that don't seem to last particularly well. I frown as I count the population a third time, certain he brought back more than the current complement.

"Of course I am. She's far from stupid." I ground my teeth together. Gella wanted to tempt Amy into the open, but I knew better than to bring the demoness to my home. Sorceress. Demoness. Whatever the witch wanted to be called. "She'll see straight through the ruse the moment she arrives, if she hasn't already. It's not like she doesn't believe that my wife has connected all the hints she's laid out."

"Truth be told, I'll be glad when this is over." Dolion sighed, staring across the yard to where

Minette helped Gella play quoits in the darkness, their path lit by a circle of lanterns.

The affair looked less like a morning game held after dinner than a séance, but my wife insisted on sleeping and waking the same hours as I did.

"Is my bellyaching so great?" I looked at him sharply. "When are you going to confess to diddling my maid?"

Dolion's stone façade creased. "Do you have to be so...colonial?"

"We live in the new world," I reminded him, though my heart panged. The thought of returning to France occurred to me, taking Gella back but...I wasn't welcome there any more than I was here, in this country with its new superstitions and old gods.

"We do," he sighed. "I miss haunting the buildings, Sebastian. Staring down at ancient, cobbled streets, the partygoers trampling filth beneath their heeled shoes. Glorious carriages and pretty women squealing at my hideousness."

I snorted. "You should be a poet, not a gargoyle."

He barely looked my way, his gaze intent on Minette who takes her turn and misses their goal by a mile. "Is there a reason I cannot be both?"

Breath escaped me. "Be what you like, my friend. We have all the time in the world."

His answer was less than an enigmatic smile as he stretched forward, breaking through his stone-skin, and scooped one of the young catfish from the waters around him. A swallow, and the creature was gone.

"Delicious. Please have your man deliver more." He leapt off his pedestal, his clawed feet becoming more human, but not fully, as he strode toward the women who greeted him as an old friend while he played court games with them in an untried land at midnight.

My fingers itched at my side as I slowly joined them, Gella's mind brushing mine.

You're grumpy tonight, my lord.

I snarled softly inside her mind. *Since when do we use titles,* my wife?

Since you looked at me like I was the last thing on your mind.

Her eyes glowed bottomless in the flickering lantern lights.

I smirked, catching her waist. *Feeling left out?* Her shove told me I rectified that error as I wound my arms around her frail frame. So breakable.

Fragile.

Her fingers traced across my stomach over my shirt in an intimate gesture that, anywhere else, would be frowned upon, socially. Here, we had forgotten the rules of society and lived amongst our own. A pity that soon we would have to remember them all again.

My mind brushed hers as she settled against me. *Don't get comfortable, Gella. I have a fantasy I want to play out with you.*

Taking inspiration from our bayou witch, I concentrated, pushing my words along with the image of her pale feet fleeing through the maze, bare as her breath pants between pale lips. Her pulse rode hard under my fingers when I stroked her throat and I knew she got the message.

"When?" she breathed.

I looked beyond the darkness. "I'll count."

"To what?"

"I'm not sure yet." I smiled when Dolion turned a quizzical glance my way and spoke directly into the most intimate part of her mind.

Run, Gella.

She leaned into me a second longer before her shoes slipped off and she pattered away on bare feet. *One, two, three...*

Don't go too fast. Her little huffs accentuated her dilemma.

Stay, and see if my threat was good. Run, and find out how fast I could catch her.

Her internal debate might have been cute how she seemed to think sassing me would get her out of trouble, except that it won't work.

Run faster, Gella.

The smile remained on my face as Dolion stared at me, turning Minette away despite her protests.

"Come, my love. I feel Sebastian and his precious woman want their time together now. And so should we, before the sun rises." He nuzzled into her neck to the melody of her giggles, and I wondered if I need to have a chat about the birds and the stone bees with my gargoyle.

Then Gella's ragged breaths distracted me, and my

thoughts merged away from our friends as I hunted my wife like so much prey through the maze.

I'll find you, Gella. Don't bother hiding.

I heard her laughter, rather than experienced it in my head. I smile. She was closer than I expected, probably planning on doubling back, the little minx. Smart creature she was. *But sometimes clever is too clever.*

Then stop cheating, she bantered back, her voice drifting away.

Along with her presence.

I frowned, heading for the center of the maze, toward the black poppies. "Gella," I called aloud, remembering the abject fear that haunted her voice in my head the night she lost herself on these paths, and my inability to find her then. "Wait."

The game quickly turned on me. I spun in a circle, focusing on her humanity, her mortal frailty that would draw not only a hunter like myself to her this night but any other in the vicinity.

This was a terrible idea.

I rounded the corner of the tallest walls, their hedges overgrown, reaching for me as I yanked at the wayward strands, pulling a hole in a section when I found myself penned in at a dead end, and no wife in sight.

"Gella!" my voice echoed through the still night.

"I'm here, Sebastian."

I turned and there she stood, the single, pale form in a sliver of moonlight amongst shadows. Her dress pooled the ground at her feet as she stepped hesitantly from the muddle of material. Her hair hung long over her shoulders, unpinned. Those damned devices scattered the ground beneath her feet where she ripped them out, trailing the area. I'd be picking them out of my garden for weeks to come, but I didn't care.

Gisella stared up at me, her skin silvery, pristine beneath the moon's sensual kiss. Her shoulders dropped back, lifting her breasts, their heavy swell rising with each sharp breath. Dusky nipples tightened beneath my gaze, and her breath wasn't the only labored.

My need rose with her proximity. I forced myself to remain still. "Run, Gella," I whispered, so brief the night air sucks my words away. I bared my teeth and her eyes widened, fear edging in as she rocked backward, then she was gone.

But not far enough. Never far enough to escape me.

I slunk into the shadows, my panic of finding her reduced as my arousal scented hers. She might as well be dripping for all the traces she left. I let her run on, turning herself in frantic circles until she stumbled back into a path she's already used.

One I remained in, waiting.

"Sebastian," she gasped, tripping over her toes.

Her hand came up to cover her body, but I snarled, lunging in front of her in a breath, knocking her cover away.

"You will never hide from me." I dug my nails painfully into her hip, jerking her into my fully clothed body. Hells, she was as cold as alabaster. I licked a line along her cheek, tasting her tears, her fear. Her need. "Never cover yourself in front of me, unless I tell you to do so. This body. Who does it belong to?" I demanded.

"You," she whispered, a final tear, a perfect, pear-shaped dew drop trembling on her upper lashes as she stared up at me, her frightened breaths coming so much harder as she wriggled in my grasp. "Let me go."

Reminded of the catfish Dolion swallowed whole, I smiled, letting my fangs lengthen past my lips. "I want to mark you, Gella. Something you'll remember for a long time."

"W-where?" she shivered when I don't release her, backing her into a hedge taller than us both. Flag-stones turn to sand beneath our feet, the positioning perfect.

"Here." I traced her pulse beneath my thumb where her life flurried, both of us knowing I could end her in a moment. "Here." I touched the top of her breast, skating my fingertips across the creamy, perfect skin. Not after tonight; she'd bear my marks forever. "Here." I cupped my hand between her legs, thrusting two fingers inside her to coat them and smear the top of her thigh near her swollen flesh, right along the inside of the crease. "These are the places I'll mark. And you'll scream and cry and come like a wounded animal while I mark you and then fuck you until the sun rises." I fixed her with a hard look. "And after tonight you will never, *ever* run from me again."

She nodded, though her body trembled. Anticipation, terror? I couldn't tell. "Yes, my lord."

I growled at her. "Use. My. Name."

"Yes, Sebastian," she murmured, bowing her head.

I forced her chin back and claimed her mouth, pushing her onto her knees as I kneeled before her, and found that pulse point. "Hold onto me," I warned her. "This won't be sweet, not to start."

Her pulse flickered faster. *Definitely fear.* My breeches tightened as my cock roared to life. I tilted her head to the side, licking her flesh, and sank my teeth into her.

Warmth flooded my mouth, her sweet metallic tang coating my throat. I groaned as I gorged myself in a single mouthful, reminding myself I couldn't drain her. Rearing back, I bit her again, tearing her skin as she sobbed above me, scoring my shoulders with her nails.

"Sebastian," she gasped. "Stop!"

No. Tonight you are mine, no longer someone else's.

I smiled cruelly into her bloodied neck and bit her again.

And again, and again.

And when her screams of fear broke and I closed the wounds so she wouldn't bleed out on me, I started on her breasts, turning pain to pleasure until she writhed, her legs sliding open, heat gushing for me, welcoming my cock deep inside her. Those screams filled the maze, drenching the creatures who resided there that night in her scent, *our* scent.

Her body shook and trembled many times. The sun's arrival warned me of the end of my night's activities. I pressed my lips to her inner thigh, the last place I promised I'd mark, and bit deeply, bruising her skin in a way that would never heal fully while my seed still oozed from her used body.

She moaned, thrashing weakly as she tangled her hands in my hair, riding the waves of pleasure from my bite.

"Pain, need, pleasure. The three things I offer in my bed, Gella. I never asked your permission to marry. I never gave you those promises myself. But I promise you this, now. While ever I exist and you roam this place, I will protect you. Wear my marks and you are mine. I'll give my immortal existence for you, Gella. Everything I am is yours. For you." My voice cracked, and I returned to drinking, slower, savoring her.

I couldn't take more without killing her, but I satisfied myself with licking the wound clean, then turning to her swollen flesh I bruised in a different way earlier and licked and sucked until she cried and screamed herself hoarse.

Then, before the sun crested above the horizon, I carried her into the house and pulled all the drapes shut, falling into a dreamless sleep with Gella curled in my arms.

CHAPTER TWENTY

GISELLA

I stretched my cramped fingers and placed the quill on the polished wooden desk. Sebastian picked it up, sharpening its tattered end with a small knife.

"Why don't you do some?" I yawned, still massaging my hand.

Tremors ran along its length from overuse. I pressed my palm flat to the cold surface of the desk, the coolness easing my aching muscles. Dozens of invitations and menus lay drying across the front of the broad desk.

We'd ensconced ourselves in the large, downstairs library Sebastian never seemed to use, but was decorated with evidence of his 'human' life—a sextant, a portrait he painted himself, though the ones upstairs in my room and the gallery were much better. That did seem to happen when one had centuries to improve on a skill. And that was the room we stayed in to work through the lists as quick as possible.

Even so, the light was beginning to intrude on our scant hours together.

"But you're doing such a wonderful job," he murmured, returning the pointed quill to me. "Besides, you've seen my attempts."

I nodded, eyeing the crumpled papers littering the other end of the desk. While Sebastian could speak fluent English, his written form was sharp and disjointed. Amazingly, his written French was decorated with beautiful curvatures and flourishes.

"Fine, how many more to go?"

"If you're going to mouth off like that, maybe I should tie you to that chair until you're done. Then I'll take that attitude out on that delicious bottom of yours." He raised an eyebrow in my direction and pushed a small pile of fine parchment toward me.

Covering the instant flush of arousal that doused me in heat, my thighs slick in an instant, I groaned and took the top leaf. "If you say so," I muttered, keeping up the attitude, just to see what he would do.

Sebastian didn't disappoint.

His fingers closed around my chin, jerking my face up to stare into his dark eyes roiling with desire and need. He loomed over me, and I hadn't even seen him move.

"I'm sorry—" I gasped, but he wasn't having it.

"You're lucky there are servants about. Otherwise, you'd be on your knees with my cock in your mouth until I found my pleasure in you, just enough to bring on the edge of your own. And when I was done, I'd leave you as a sticky, panting little mess," he growled every word, arcing his body over mine.

I think I'm already there.

I swallowed when his relentless gaze held mine as though he considered following through on his threat despite the constant staff whizzing past the library door. "I've never done—that," I whispered.

Sebastian's hard gaze softened. "I know, love. I'll teach you. One day when my patience is stronger and this is all over. I promise you I'll take the time to train you in what I need." He brushed a kiss over my parted lips, and sat back down on the other side of the desk like he hadn't almost had me on my knees a second before.

I sucked in a shaky breath, and pulled the next invitation toward me. Several dozen later, he shifted in his seat, the motion of a man whose patience had indeed run through.

"I'll leave you for a few hours, Gella. Get Charleton to—"

"I know how to organize a ball, Sebastian," I snapped, then covered my face with my hands. "I didn't mean that. I mean, I do, but— oh, I'm sorry."

Firm hands closed around my shoulders, rubbing to my neck. I wondered if he would throw me over the desk and take what he needed from my hide, but instead he continued his massage. Pops and cracks burst from my shoulders as he manipulated my upper body. I leaned back against him as his fingers dipped into the top of my bodice.

I pressed my hands over his, unwilling to give any more time to the job at hand but knowing it needed to be done for the plan to work, even if it meant sacrificing precious moments like these.

"If we don't get this done, we won't have a ball. How do we know she'll come?" I tilted my head to look up at him.

He stared back at me with fierce eyes, and I was glad I wouldn't be on the other end of his fury this time.

"She'll come."

I was halfway through the stack when Sebastian put himself to bed. Charleton fed me at appropriate intervals, and I was grateful to be able to exchange the completed tower of invitations intended for local families for a small platter of morsels. Charleton and Minette had made a list for us of the names in town. It turned out the staff knew most of the town, though that didn't surprise me. We weren't as isolated as I had initially thought. I handed him a few extra notices to put up in the local trading post.

Charleton balanced them on one arm and managed to pour me thick, black coffee at the same time.

"You're a gem, Charleton. Thank you." He nodded, his mouth opening and closing. I blinked. "Have I forgotten something?"

"Things will change after this, won't they?"

We'd filled Charleton in on our plan—omitting the part about Amy's planned demise. I balked still at the thought of planning something so dark, while Sebastian hadn't so much as batted an eyelid. He withdrew his brooding presence from myself and the household by the day.

"Yes. I suspect they will."

Charleton nodded again, taking my completed invitations away. I watched him leave, foreboding roiling in my belly. I hadn't been able to settle since we'd returned from the bayou, except for those few stolen moments in Sebastian's arms.

The valet had indeed outdone himself in service to his master. And to me, I supposed. Charleton organized the staff, telling them what was coming and what we expected of them all, in terms of service. I suspected this ball would be less like any other the area had seen—if the fledgling town had even held one before.

I sank back in the bath, letting the water take my weight and my muscles uncoil themselves from the knots my shoulders had wound themselves into. Leaning over the desk writing out adverts and invitations hadn't been good for my posture. I stretched out, learning to paddle across the pool on my own. In a different place the skill might have made me outcast or worse as a witch, but drifting in the pool was one of the activities I looked forward to once the sun rose, and Sebastian retreated from the day.

But it wasn't the same without him during the day —being here with him had become my peace, my sanctuary. As it had been his for the years here, I suspected. I wondered what he had done in France to relax? I needed to remember to ask him.

He'd had some errand to do during his waking hours, mumbling something that sounded rather like *Dolion* and *wolves*, launching himself from the second story balcony to land onto the drive with barely a crunch of gravel. He disappeared into the garden as a blur—I was still getting my mind around who he was and how his body worked. *Lived.*

I frowned, searching for him; usually, I could still feel him in my mind, but perhaps he didn't want me listening in on his conversations with Granny Smythe and her pack. The wolves might have let us go to her, but I got the feeling we weren't particularly welcome to drop by at any random time.

I leaned back, letting my hair trail in the water, and closed my eyes. In the semi-darkness of the pool-cave, I was able to let go.

Do you miss him, Gisella?

I shot upright, water streaming from my arms. Wet hair hung in a long stream down my back.

"Amy?" I whispered with no small dose of horror, her name echoing across the ripples in the pool. "How are you in my head?"

Inside, I screamed, and I supposed she could hear

that, too. But this was my private place, with Sebastian. Where we rediscovered each other, after his absence and my...disobedience.

The word sat poorly in my mouth, but I considered it, turning the thought over. But he demanded it, and I gave to him freely, submitting to his will, enjoying it.

If I asked something of him, would I want *his* obedience? According to our current laws—even the unfortunate ones New Orleans inherited from France —I had no right to such a thought. But I suspected Sebastian, having experienced so much in his overly long life, was different.

Was I being too outlandish, too modern in my thoughts?

Not to me...Gella. Is that what he calls you? How quaint.

"Get out," I whispered, my senses hyperalert. I turned in circles, but she wasn't in the room with me.

But she had taken up residence in my head without my permission.

I wasn't sure what was worse. Would I ever be able to sleep without either of them talking inside my mind, or keep my secrets? *His* secrets?

She laughed, a brittle thing, her sarcasm bouncing off the walls encasing my mind, though she had purred my name a moment before, like a lover.

You'd know something of that by now, surely, about your husband? You were so beautifully naive.

"Get *OUT!*" I screamed, my vocal cords straining with the effort, breaking at the end. "You're never welcome here. Anitta." I used the name Sebastian had given me, hoping it would banish her behind a door of her own making.

Her mocking laugh tinkled in my head.

No such luck.

He did do the thing properly, didn't he? Well, I'm sure I'll be back.

I blinked, and my mind was my own again. Her presence had vanished with the last, faint echoes of my screams.

I didn't tell Sebastian about Amy's intrusion into my waking hours. I couldn't. Everything we planned was based on a being, an entity, who he seemed to understand. I was the weak link, the mortal amongst monsters. *Monsters who love.* I could muse the point all day, but it wouldn't get anything constructive done.

Bolts of fabric in several shades of complementing blues and one horrible mustard-yellow lay across my lap. I fingered one of deepest blue while Minette removed the others, replacing them with a cream lace and a silver trim ribbon. I smiled, discarding the lace for the first time in my life, and handed the ribbon back to her.

"What style would you like, madame?"

I shot her a hard look. She held my eye before giggles erupted from her lips. She was an infectious creature, and soon my sides ached. I pressed a hand to my stomach, waving her away as shadows lengthened across the floor. Sebastian opted to sleep in the prelude to the ball. Whether to renew his strength or for the simple solitude to meditate, it was unclear.

Something he hadn't let me in on while I was left to plan the remainder of the event.

"You pick, Minette. I trust your choices. How's James?" I asked, off-hand, folding the ribbon back into its packet.

Minette turned a sweet shade of pink.

"He—ah, he's been...well. I think," she mumbled into an armful of material raised suspiciously high.

I sighed and pressed my hand to the top of the pile until her eyes became visible.

"What happened?" I asked softly.

"Nothing!" She gave me a startled glance and scurried from the room.

I shook my head, still clutching the ribbon, and placed it beside the bed for her to find later. Amusement niggled inside my head that wasn't my own, and I sighed, eager to see Sebastian. Maybe I'd have to start reversing my days and nights after all.

Oh, I wouldn't get too excited, Gella. I'm sure he's hours away from breaking his own thoughts.

My teeth clenched at Amy's intrusion. Would I have to get used to her in my own headspace, too? Gone were the days of privacy, then.

"I told you to get out," I groused through gritted teeth. My jaw ached from the constant, restrained tension until I was fit to bust. I sucked in a breath, my cheeks depressing against my teeth with the effort. "You have no place here."

I carved out the thought in a resolute manner, hoping with no little dose of desperation she'd get the hint, but I doubted it would work.

But I need to be here. For him. For you.

I ignored that, collecting books from my dresser and heading for the library. Our little library, between our rooms. I needed to ask Sebastian how to block unwelcome thoughts, but without explaining why. That could be difficult.

Yes, I rather think it will be.

Her amusement irked me. I threw up a rude image I'd seen the sailors on the docks throw to one another in jest, but sent mine with the greatest effort of disgust I could manage. If Amy had any sinful crutch beside lust, it was pride. I could work with that.

The barb worked—a little too well.

I grabbed for the handle of my door, but my muscles refused to move. Even my feet were frozen where I stood. I gaped—or tried to—but my mouth seemed glued shut, too.

"Is this you?" I hissed through numbed lips, my words slurring together horribly.

Of course, silly. How else was I to get you alone?

"Why?" I didn't bother with extra words. The mumbling would serve to amuse her and humiliate me.

Smart little thing, aren't you now?

My feet turned of their own accord, walking me

back to the bed. I watched in abject horror as my body became a marionette on invisible strings with me trapped within. But she hadn't numbed all of me. I could still feel—everything. Under her guidance, my fingers trailed the ribbon, lacing it around my wrist.

I think you'll get the idea soon.

My knees hit the bed in a jarring motion as though she hadn't got this puppeteering thing down pat, just yet. I felt rather than heard her sneer in my head, but she didn't allow that small backstep to prevent her from moving forward with her plans.

I watched my hand rise, reaching up to my neck, coiling the length of ribbon around and around. Once, then twice. I swallowed beneath it, my airway already restricted.

"Are you going to kill me?" I gasped out, my words mingling on top of each other.

I had the impression of her smiling. Then my other hand caught the remaining end, forming a knot I couldn't have made if it were in front of me.

Then, my hands pulled.

Blood suffused my face instantly, bringing with them heat and a panic I'd never experienced, not even when my deranged father had sent me from my filial home. Not when my mother had died.

I had no control over what Amy was doing to me with my own body. It was the grossest form of invasion.

Hands wrapped tight in ribbon, my wrists and neck battled for the honor of which was trussed tightest. I tried to swallow and couldn't; saliva dribbled from my lips as Amy departed, her laugh tinkling in my ears. I pitched face first into a lump of bedclothes.

Unable to get a breath in or out, the ribbon cut into my throat as my hands drew it ever tighter. The soft, silver ribbon became a garrote that sliced into my wrists. Tears streamed from my eyes, wetting the already uncomfortable hot mass of sheets and quilts.

Why would she kill me? Because of Sebastian? Questions I thought we'd already answered swirled in my mind, my eyes watering with the heat of my face. If I didn't choke to death in my own bile and saliva on the ribbon, I'd asphyxiate, stuck in the swath of material I'd tumbled into.

What a sight I must make, rump in the air, face pressed down on the bed. Sebastian would find me a sight, I was sure. And perhaps he would be relieved. My mind numbed, along with my wrists, and my throat. A serenity stole over me, and I let my eyes flutter closed. In this, as with him, I let my body and mind submit.

You trained me too well, husband.

I managed a brief smile at my state of deshabille, and sank into nothingness.

I THINK NO SUCH THING!

Hands gripped my ribs with force, tossing me onto my back. I blinked lazy eyes, staring into the pale face that wouldn't quite come into focus. Something humorous about one man finding me in his bed with another crossed my mind, but it was gone before I could process it. My eyes drifted shut again.

"Goddamn you, Gella! Let go of this—let *go*. Gella. You have to let go." Fear mingled in a cold rage that coated his words, but it was the former that drew me back to him.

Fear for...me?

I blinked at the tugging on my fingers, trying to look down but everything was stuck. Sebastian slid into focus above me, and I marveled at him. *So beautiful.*

Thank you, but let's get you freed first, love. Then we can deal with the pleasantries.

His victory rolled through me as the ribbon was stripped away from my hands, torn from my throat. With it, mobility returned, and my body was once again under my own control. Amy's presence dropped far distant from my mind. I beamed my gratitude as my fogged brain was certain I should for a single second.

Then, sensation returned.

Pain burst at every point in my hands, my fingers stabbed with a thousand needles. I gasped on my back, flopping to bring air into my flattened throat, a displaced fish with no pond to rescue me. He rolled me onto my front, and I fell into the bedclothes once more. In less than a second, panic set in.

I thrashed in the tangle of sheets, heat rushing into my face again. I couldn't breathe. Sebastian hauled me upright, holding me away from his body as I gulped air.

"You're all right, Gella. It's okay." His fingers

hovered between my wrists and throat but never touching.

I imagined the marks torn into my skin. Blessedly, a numbness stole over the areas, and I rasped in thin draws of air. His arms wrapped around me, pulling me into him this time, but still cautious of my neck. I burrowed into him, glad of his scent, of the safety his embrace offered.

"What happened?" He cupped my elbow, drawing me back. "Gella? Do you not want to...be here?" His tone guarded, he surveyed me with a critical eye.

"Don't look," I wheezed, "I'm a mess."

"You're beautiful. But why?" His eyes turned hard, his face like granite.

"What?" I gaped, glad to be able to move as I pleased. Something deep inside me quailed at the thought she might be back, to ruin me further, but I pushed the thought aside to address later. "Do you think I did this myself?"

He gestured to the bedclothes; the ribbon lumped in a tangle upon itself. I recoiled from the thing in horror, tears pricking my eyes as he allowed me to burrow back into him.

Gella. If you can't tell me, will you show me?

I nodded miserably into his shirt, tears blotting the thin material, and slid my head to the side, despite the deep ache in my neck. Things not so physical hurt inside me; the surface wounds were the least of my worries.

He sucked in a breath above me, his fingers sliding into my hair, his touch tender as he kissed my skin. Working in slow steps, he dipped his head, lips pressing gently, oh so gently, against the wound I hadn't made. Or maybe I had, with my struggles. I waited for the sharp pain of his bite, but he soothed the wound with his tongue, cradling me to him as he took me back through the last few minutes, though it had felt so much longer.

I watch the events of the last moments—what could have been *my* last moments—dispassionately. Numbness drenched my soul.

My memories slid across my vision that I knew he shared, a live stage play of my own life. Every word Amy had said came out spoken, as though she'd said the word out loud, not lodged inside the dark edges of my mind.

Through it, Sebastian held me to him, his lips pressed to my skin as he took the smallest amount from me. When I watched his hands touch my waist, he squeezed me, raising his head. The memory disappeared in a rush, and with it, a finality of sorts settled into my awareness.

I blinked.

"What did you do?"

"I shut her out. I think. I've tried to mirror the—what is it you say about my presence?— a void."

"When she goes into my head, she will encounter a —a wall?" My brow furrowed.

I tried to work out what he meant, but the concept

of seeing my own mind from someone else's point of view appeared to be beyond me.

Sebastian brushed his fingers over the lines forming there, smoothing them. "She won't be able to find your mind at all, assuming I've done it right. You won't be...visible to her at all."

"Can you still speak to me? Like you have been?"

You mean, in here?

A shiver ran through me at his presence there, like it had been between us, before. Not an intrusion, but safe, and...all him. *Sebastian.* My cheeks heated as I smiled shyly. Pain flared across my throat again, taking any thoughts of time together with it.

"I don't want to be like that. Like...her."

You mean like me.

Pure pain laced his voice, ricocheting through my head, but neither of us bothered to deny the truth of the statement, the disquiet that rose in my throat as a silent scream I trapped beneath layer after layer of love and hurt and all the things we were together, who we had become.

Because this mortal life was all I could give him. It would have to be enough, because it was all I had.

Then, he would wander on into an unknown destination alone. I wouldn't-could *not* risk- becoming like her. Nothing like her. I'd seen what the curse of immortality did to a mind, and I did not want its kiss, or its temptation.

"I'm sorry," I whispered, my vision blurring before me.

"No, Gella. It is I who am sorry. For everything. But I, too, am selfish for not being sorry to drag you here and stealing the years of your mortal life to share with you."

Tenderly reclining me back onto my pillow, he stared into my eyes for a moment, then strode to my door. I blinked back tears at his sudden exit, but voices murmured from the hall. He returned swiftly, sliding his arms around me, pulling me into his strength.

Rest, Gella. Let me care for the horrors I've inflicted on you.

I blinked, wanting to tell him that they weren't his horrors, that none of this was his fault at all, but exhaustion threw a blanket over me, and I sank into the familiar nothingness of him.

CHAPTER TWENTY-ONE

GISELLA

In the space of a few short weeks, the austere, though luxurious, interior of Sebastian's castle—I refused to call it anything else now—transformed into something magical. The townspeople talked about nothing else, according to bavardage my maid peddled from downstairs.

Outside, everything appeared perfect. Excitement carried on the wind, and even Granny Smythe's wolf-men acknowledged the event.

On the inside, panic reigned. Staff flurried about the house sorting decorations and polishing silver after weeks of planning. Sebastian brought what must have been centuries worth of the royal service collection with him when he'd left France. Dresses were laid out, altered and restyled. Minette met any ladies who considered themselves seamstresses or who possessed any such skills in the town, and collected as many bolts of fabric as possible.

The trading post was alit with the news of a ball at the house, and no one was permitted to enter except for the staff. The ballroom was scrubbed until the black and white tiles I had encountered on my first day in Sebastian's home that he imported from France, along with the rest of his belongings, glowed with the shimmering reflection of the chandelier above, and the silver vines glinted in the reflected crystalline light.

Minette laid out the gown she'd stitched for me, and I marveled at her talents. The dress consisted of two flowing swathes of a translucent blue material that faded to cream at the bottom. A deep vee mirrored both back and front, with a gathered waist that flowed to the floor in a sweeping bell shape.

A matching mask of deep blue lace covered my eyes, fading to the same cream as the dress as it descended to my cheeks. She'd designed a thin choker of the same, deep blue to cover the lines still visible around my throat from my torture, and silver cuffs with bows draped my wrists.

"You've done...an incredible job, Minette." I twirled in place, a little giddy at the finery.

Minette bobbed a courtesy, a blush rising in her cheeks. She straightened the blue feathers she'd intertwined through my hair, which tumbled around them in a confection of curls laced with a length of silver ribbon.

Her own uniform for the evening had been altered,

as had all the staff's. Black lace edges were applied to all their service wear, with velvet as the distinguishing feature on Charleton's coat. Each wore a prominent black mask across their eyes in the shape of the *fleur-de-lys*.

"You look beautiful, madame." Minette opened the door, ushering me through, still refusing to call me by my preferred name.

"As do you," I smiled. Minette's tiny curls framed her head with a blonde halo. I stepped into the hall and ran into Sebastian's chest. "Do you have to be so close?" I grumbled, rubbing my forehead as I looked up at him.

My mouth dried as I stared at the imposing figure who reminded me of the mysterious man I had encountered on my first day in his home before I knew his name. Sebastian's face was half-covered by a black, velvet mask, and he was dressed head to toe in black: breeches, stockings, and boots, with a short, evening cape that swirled about his shoulders as he stepped back from him.

In short, he looked like something out of a dream.

His gaze caught mine, blotting out the rest of the world.

In my periphery, Minette edged away, her feet pattering on the thick carpet as she made her escape along the hall while I froze in place, as unable to move as I had been that first day.

Sebastian brushed my chin with the lightest touch.
My bedroom. Now.

I gave a half-laugh, hiccupping. Sebastian slid a glass of champagne into my hand, the bubbles going straight to my head. I shook it; I needed to be in control of my thoughts tonight.

Do you?

"You are the highest form of temptation," I murmured, sipping the delicate bubbles. Memories of France rushed over me, my home, my mother before I lost her. I shook the images away. No distractions were allowed tonight; none at all. We had to focus on our task.

Tilting my head back to offer some snarky remark about places and times, I made the mistake of losing myself in my husband's fathomless gaze.

You're not objecting, wife.

"Not tonight."

Sebastian's hand slid around my waist, pressing against the small of my back as he drew me impossibly close. My throat closed on a breath until his strange presence enveloped me.

"Shall we?" he asked, his eyes dark beneath his mask as he surveyed me. His sinful smile promised tantalizing fantasies that crossed my mind in a montage of debauchery.

A shiver raced over my skin. He could pull off any of those acts; I knew that from first-hand experience. I nodded, unable to answer him.

Matching his steps as we moved through the hall together, I tried to concentrate on tonight's performance, running a list through my head of everything important, already acknowledging it was too late as the guests had started to arrive.

The silence of the upper floor clashed with a murmur from below that grew in volume with every step.

We reached the top of the stairs to find a steady line of people entering the ballroom from the foyer door. Chatter filled the lower levels of the house. I inhaled slowly, subduing the desire to race back to my room and close the door. Lock it, maybe. I sipped my champagne then on impulse drained the glass, leaving it on a side table.

Guests in costumes and finery mingled around columns dressed in Sebastian's colors. New Orleans rose to the moment for our masquerade ball.

Combined with the sense of impending disaster that encompassed me, it was all a little too overwhelming. I flapped about for Sebastian's hand with an edge of desperation, needing to anchor to something solid. He held out his arm, and I clung to it.

Breathe, Gella. It will be over soon. You don't have to do anything.

But you...will.

I squeezed my eyes shut and forced my feet forward. The illusion of solitude fell away, the crowd rushing back with a roar that drew an ache from the back of my head. I rubbed it, something niggling there.

"Easy for you to say, when you've had a target from an ancient hedge witch painted on your behind," I muttered.

But it's such a lovely behind, wife. I enjoy using it for my own pleasure.

I flushed.

Sebastian laughed as we reached the bottom of the stairs. Heads turned in our direction, searching for the source and settled on us. I refused to shrink beneath all those pairs of eyes, though I desperately wanted to return to my bed—or his—and never emerge again.

At least, until they all left.

I've been away from people for too long already.

A large shape blocked the sea of eyes from my line of sight. I blinked at Dolion, dressed in a finely-tailored suit of red and black.

"You're wearing clothes," I blurted.

A fresh flush decorated my face as both of my monsters laughed. I shook my head in mock despair, letting their easy humor sweep away my fears for the moment.

A group of men with long hair, dressed in leathers appeared in the doorway to my side. Sebastian stiffened as they parted to reveal Granny Smythe looking anything but Granny-like in a stunningly simple gown of black, shimmery material. Knowing something of her age, if not the exact date, I had to admit the ancient creature aged spectacularly.

Sebastian sighed, squeezing my arm as he went to address his guest.

"You've quite outdone yourself," Dolion murmured in my ear, bending low to speak to me. "Tonight will be a grand success. All will be well." He straightened, linking back to our previous conversation in a louder voice designed to carry. "Yes, Minette appeared to enjoy the measuring process," Dolion offered me his arm and led me into the ballroom.

Guests parted before the dark-skinned giant as we progressed through the crowd. Murmurs of rumors I expected reached me, but none seemed malicious. In fact, most party-goers appeared awestruck, and as I drew my attention back to the center of the ballroom, I understood their perception of the castle.

Black velvet draped from the ceiling in long rows, with a flicker of blue in between the wide swathes of material. Charleton had somehow stained the vines climbing the columns a brighter silver, so they reflected the sea of color swarming beneath in an ever-undulating mass.

I wondered if Minette hadn't designed the color scheme as well as my dress and the uniforms.

"You seem quite taken with my maid," I observed, watching him track Minette's head of blonde curls bob her way across the room, collecting empty trays and glasses. "When did you take your measurements? Have you been keeping my staff up at all hours?" I teased, taking a fresh glass of champagne from a tray Minette offered with a genuine smile, albeit aided by the bubbles of the last glass.

Keep your head about you, wife.

Minette's eyes lingered on Dolion for a long moment before she resumed her duties.

"Not at all," he replied, watching her sashay away

in her adjusted uniform, lace brushing the backs of her calves in a break in protocol. The masks gave everyone a chance to feel the fantasy that flowed through the event, and the staff were not immune from the magical feel of the night. "She's been visiting me in the garden, bringing me lunch. Now that we appear to be out in the open, it is much easier to have...friends."

"Friends who are human," I said softly, the implications of my limited mortality hitting me.

I had been so busy planning, I'd allocated little energy to process the intricacies of my relationship with a relative immortal. And what was true for Sebastian and me, was likely also true for others.

"Yes," Dolion's gaze weighed heavily on me.

A hand slipped around my waist, the touch so familiar, his silent presence so undeniable that I knew who touched me. I leaned back into my husband's broad chest.

"Please, mingle with my staff," his voice resonated with all the unspoken things of the night as he spoke over my head.

Dolion turned his weighted stare on his friend and loped away into the crowd who parted for the huge man.

"Is she here, yet?" I asked softly, though the chatter of so many people in the ballroom filled the space and reverberated against the walls.

"Not yet—" His face shut down, and I spun around as the crowd parted for a pale woman dressed in a burgundy gown that flowed behind her in a long train.

I stared past Amy for her husband, the young man who met her at the docks, but she appeared to be alone.

I wondered if she had killed him already…or worse.

"Gisella," she cried in farce, sliding her arms around me in an embrace.

"Amy," I croaked the name, but no one seemed to notice my failure. I remembered to smile, to play the part, that she knew nothing of our plans. Didn't she? My stomach coiled back on itself, defiance and betrayal warring in a duel that drew my attention from our greatest foe in the room. But we had a plan, and I would go with it, until it failed us. Then…

It took everything I had not to recoil from her touch. Amy's fingers dragged over the choker Minette made up for me to cover her marks, and Sebastian's. "But you look so beautiful."

I murmured something inconsequential. My heart racing, I released her as soon as was socially acceptable, presenting Sebastian in a recited monotone. It was all so *fake*. We'd agreed to continue the pretense for as long as possible, as that's what she would expect. Sebastian had detailed to me a hundred encounters where conversations were held at both vocal and mind levels during events, with society none the wiser. I had been flabbergasted, and still struggled to grasp the concept.

"Where is your lovely young man?" A pathetic attempt at conversation, but the most I could manage as my brain jammed.

"Oh, you know, he was so sweet, I simply *devoured* him." She turned eyes full of mirth on me.

My stomach curled on itself again as I wondered at the reality of her comment. Any more of this and I would retch champagne all over the well-polished floor. My pale reflection stared back at me in the tile's glossy sheen. Amy joined me, her smile widening. I half expected her face to morph into something demonic, but her sugar-sweet smile remained innocent beside my frozen reflection, denying the demoness hidden beneath.

Unable to focus around her, my mind whirled, as though her presence alone poisoned my ability to think. To each side of us, I noted the gargoyle and the wolves gathered. As one they moved, an escort of pure muscle, herding us toward the drive.

No, Amy was no fool. She took a bait I never offered and I stepped into her trap, along with everyone in this place that I loved.

My mouth opened to scream, call for help, but even my brain behaved like sludge, unable to ask for the aid I so desperately needed.

Do you not think I don't know what you've done, Gisella?

The voice inside my head was snide, but it wasn't Sebastian's. Neither was it welcome. I struggled to stay upright, clinging to his arm as Amy continued to chatter inanely at both of us at once.

I dragged my attention to the guests who milled around the foyer and the drive, noting the opaque, out of focus eyes. While my mind tried to comprehend what that meant, Sebastian gripped my arm tight, drawing me toward the house.

Go, Gella.

Urgency lit his tone as he pushed me back in a violent gesture that left me reeling. I stumbled, turning in the direction he expected, but the wolves circled us on each side, preventing any escape. A deep rumble grew in his chest, and I knew his fury wouldn't be contained any longer.

Even Granny Smythe's wolf-men were captivated by Amy's brand of darkness and magic. For all their muscle and authority, their eyes stared blankly, opaque, and I knew they were not themselves.

"How many conversations can you hold at once, Amy?" I gasped, my thoughts lining up long enough for me to make sense of the situation.

I needed a distraction and flung around for ideas with my fogged mind. Beside me, Dolion slipped into our circle, his skin yellowing, hardening to his stone form in preparation for the confrontation that had to occur.

My hands trembled as I gripped the coat arms of the men I adored either side of me. A single thought sliced through my mind that floored me, raw and desperate. Neither was it a private link with Sebastian, which meant everyone linked to us must have heard my internal cry.

Sebastian bent to press his lips to the top of my head without breaking eye contact with Amy.

I love you too, Gella.

A tinkle of laughter filled the courtyard, grating on my very skin with its wrongness. "Oh, many, darling girl. Did you think me as vapid as you? As mortal?" She laughed again, a sound less like bells, more shattered glass on silver, edged with a stain of something dark and dripping.

My vision swam, shadows clashing across it. I shook my head, stumbling even as I stood still. Something cold slid against my hand. My sight cleared as I looked down, away from Amy, as though looking at her directly set off some sort of defensive reaction.

Or aggressive.

I remembered Granny Smythe's words as she'd unwrapped the same tarot cards she'd read in her house. My stomach gave a lurch, water surging beneath my feet though we were no longer on the ship.

It's taking her.

I curled my toes within my blue and silver slippers that were never meant to be worn outside the comforts of the ballroom. I gripped the ground through the delicate material, determined to stay in the moment, to not be swept away as I had last time, lost to the beckoning waters.

I glanced at the ageless witch for help but her eyes were opaque, unfocussed.

Amy had stolen her, too.

Our list of allies grew thin, despite their physical presence. Without their minds, they were no more than puppets, listless marionettes, as I had been when

Amy had bid me take my own life in the house behind us.

We will not survive this.

I listened for Sebastian's easy answer, but my plea went unanswered.

CHAPTER TWENTY-TWO

GISELLA

A point dug into my skin, scratching me enough to draw a sharp gasp from my lips. I covered the pain filled sound with a cough, disguising the slip, lest Amy notice us. Hopefully she had enough conversations running about her head to not notice my *faux pas*.

The knife slipped from Sebastian's sleeve, dropping into his hand. Before I could argue, he lunged forward without so much as a step backward in preparation. I saw for the first time what an efficient killer he made. The blade, a curved, horrid thing, left his hand and circled through the air, aimed in a neat line at Amy.

A wry smile crossed her pretty face, and she shook her head as though berating wayward children who had stepped out of line. She raised a hand, and the thing flung back toward us.

Dolion lurched, steel glancing from his stone chest

in a clatter and clang. The knife bounced off him and disappeared into the hedge.

Amy turned her back to us, presenting an opportunity I knew Sebastian wouldn't waste. He blurred forward, leaping in an inhuman lurch as he had the night on the jetty. Red mixed with black, swirling around each other.

I pressed forward, but my own movements were sluggish, caught in a web Amy had spun around me while I processed events too far from my frame of reference to understand as Sebastian and Dolion did.

Around me, arms began to raise. Everything moved so slowly, I knew we would never reach the two entwined in their deadly battle before one met their end. While their movements were at such an unfathomable speed, ours were lethargic. I closed my eyes, never having imagined the limitlessness of Amy's power.

Wind whipped around us in a maelstrom of grit and silver. Then the air cleared, and Amy stood before me. Sebastian lay unmoving at her feet. Immobilized as I had been before by her hand, I couldn't even reach out for him.

Grief clogged my throat, making my next breath as impossible as the ones that never left his body. *Can an already dead man bleed?* I didn't know the answer to that question, or any other.

Her magic tightened around me, crippling at such proximity. If I had thought her powerful when she had me wrap my own neck in a noose from a distance, it had nothing on the raw strength she had in person.

How could I not see what you were when I lived beside you for months on end?

I screamed the words inside my head until she shut down that, too, deadening my fear to a muffled echo. Red lips parted in a wide smile and the tongue that licked them was anything but human.

"I shall enjoy devouring you, too," she purred. Her lithe fingers hooked into claws, reaching for me.

My stomach roiled, but death might be preferable to a life without the man I loved. "I can't fight you," I whispered, numbed lips slurring the words.

Her smile widened, long fangs extending past her lips.

And I loved you, too.

A crunch on gravel drive gave her pause, the sound originating from behind her. So out of place in the midst of her conquest, the small patter of slippered feet halted Amy's movement. Her head turned, refocusing on the newcomer.

I blinked, part of her spell easing away in her distraction. She revolved on her heel to display Minette, a vague smile on her sweet face, offering up a tray of champagne. Her eyes hooded, docile in her dreamlike state. She wobbled toward Amy over the loose stones, all expression removed from her face.

I stared at her wildly; how could she have missed what was happening here? Had Charleton been remiss in his instructions? Amy had gotten into everyone's head, even the wolves. What could I expect of the staff who had no defense from such an unknown, powerful force?

I'm so sorry.

I will take it all, Gisella. He was never worth it. And you will see.

Our thoughts collided, the words mingling into an insensible knot inside my mind. Ignoring Minette, Amy raised her arms over her head, her nails elongating into vicious talons that glowed and smoked as she gloated at me. Heat emanated from Minette's direction. The glasses bubbled and overflowed, and I knew Amy had her hand in what happened to my poor maid.

She stood vapid and relaxed, as though the liquid she carried wasn't boiling on her tray. Orange flame flashed in the crystal glasses, and they shattered as one in a cacophony that drowned out Amy's horrible laughter. Glass struck Minette's face, slicing into her flawless skin in a thousand cuts, but still, she didn't react.

The fire bloomed into a hideous thing of many heads, slicing through the crowd and felling wolves in its haste to engulf the house. The man beside shifted, did, or tried to. Dolion's stunted roar mingled with the scream of glass as it flung outward in every direction.

Minette's eyes cleared, and she sent a single, hard look in Dolion's direction.

She slipped her hand from beneath her tray, a thin, honed blade in her palm, and swept it in a wide arc.

Red flung in a hundred directions, mingling with the shattered glass as her as the knife buried itself in Amy's neck.

Scarlett, not of the sorcerer's dress, coated her skin. Her arms windmilled, smoking talons flashing as she fell, and a fresh spray of life coated my face. One slowed instance, and an eternal life was snuffed from their earth with no one left to mourn her passing.

I stared down at my husband, so still by my feet. Smoke poured around us, obscuring everything.

My eyes watered. I covered my eyes and mouth with limbs and a mind that were my own again. Relief came in the form of my own freedom until the horror around us sank into my awareness.

Screams ricocheted from the drive as people rushed from the house that billowed smoke and flame as though the very demons of hell itself walked the earth. I caught glimpses of faces blackened with soot and eyes white with fear as the townsfolk tore away from the house, Sebastian's name on too many lips.

We sought to save ourselves, but instead I have condemned you.

I closed my eyes, stumbling forward. "I'm sorry, Sebastian." It wouldn't matter if he were dead. Charleton wouldn't speak out about his master; his loyalty ran true. Dolion would run, without his friend as a solid base to rely upon. Grief bloomed in my heart.

But I loved you.

"I love you, too." Sebastian wheezed at my feet, lumbering to his knees.

That seemed to be as far as he could go for the moment, but for me, it was more than enough. I flung myself at him, rocking us both back almost to the pebbles scattered with blood and smoke.

"She killed you!" I might have screamed the words at him in my head and aloud at the same time. He winced, but I didn't care. "I watched you fall. You weren't breathing." Tears tracked down my face, heating on my skin from the flames that devoured the house behind us.

"I don't breathe, Gella." His expression lightened with a crooked smile. "It's hard to kill someone that's already dead."

I nodded, sobbing and choking the unused grief that bubbled over as my fear dissipated. "It's done?' I gasped. "She's gone?" I tried to turn around, but Sebastian held me tight.

"No, don't look," he murmured. "It's done. You're free."

I peered up at him. "And you?" *Are we still safe, together?*

Sebastian smiled. *Always, Gella.*

The last of the guests ran screaming down the hill as I huddled into his chest.

"Well, that's a whole new problem," Sebastian sighed. "Which continent would you like to try next? Dolion?"

The stone man didn't answer, and in one brief moment of clarity, I knew I had used my grief too early.

I cried out for the stone man, but he said nothing as I stumbled through smoke, tripping over the bodies of wolves, though I never spotted Granny Smythe amongst them.

"This will require quite the cleanup." Charleton appeared at my side.

He rolled bodies, checking each for signs of life as I made my way through the knot of horror Amy's darkness had brought upon us. Turning in circles, I still couldn't find the stone man.

Would he have gone back in, to check the rooms?

Being stone, I doubted fire could hurt him any more than the blade Amy tossed his way. Perhaps it had hurt him and he lay somewhere, dying. The thought of more loss broke my heart, and my tears ran fresh through the gore that covered my face.

"Dolion?" I stumbled over something solid, something warm, but wrong.

Dolion. It had to be.

Sebastian. Help me.

I felt around him, trying to lift him, but instead of a velvet suit, my hands tangled in lace, sank into a mass of ringlets, turned dark with ash and blood.

Not Minette. Anyone but her.

My friend.

"My God," I choked. My heart swelled in my chest, obliterating the scream that lodged higher up. "No—"

I told you not to swear.

"Sebastian, help me!" I whispered into her hair, tears streaming down my face.

You faced vampires and wolves and witches with me.

You met a stone man, and I think you fell in love even if you never told me.

I slid shaking hands beneath the figure below me and tried to lift her thin frame, her face waxy and covered in a hundred cuts from what she suffered to free us. Everything seemed so heavy. She slipped from my frozen hands, rolling on the gravel, listless. Lifeless. I flailed and hit something hard, tears and smoke obscuring my vision.

"I have her." Dolion's disembodied voice was muted in the hazy smoke.

Hands gripped me as I dropped to my knees, the little of the world I could see titling crazily about me.

Not Minette.

I didn't know whose thought it was, or if the grief that broke apart in my heart was mine or someone else's. The howl that reverberated inside my ears came from the man at my side.

Oh, Minette. He loved you, too.

My breath wheezed in my chest, and smoke and shadows became one.

"Gella." Sebastian's dark eyes peered in at me as though from a distance. His hair hung around his face, dark shadows smudging around his neck and shirt. His coat was nowhere to be seen. He stroked my cheek with ash smudged fingers. "Can you breathe?"

"I wouldn't be sitting up if I couldn't," I gasped, then hacked as my lungs jumped into my throat. Salty tears ran fresh down my cheeks, and God alone knew how I looked. "Wait. Minette—I found her—"

I hacked again, unable to get a full breath in, my throat raw beneath the strain of the smoke, barely recovered from the previous injury, though that no longer seemed important. His arms wound tight around me, crushing me to his chest as he turned, placing me with gentle hands on the ground at Minette's side.

Pale curls stained red framed my maid's face. A slash decorated her throat in a gruesome parody of a necklace, the edges darkened as though burned. I knew if I checked Amy's monstrous hands where she had turned her fingers into talons, I would find the same strange burns there too. Shards of crystal from the champagne glasses lodged deep in Minette's serene face. No new blood ran from her wounds, her body as still as Sebastian's at daybreak.

Dolion knelt beside her, his hand hovering over her chest, unmoving. Every inch of him had turned to stone, his expression untwisted and so much more... human.

"Dolion?" I whispered, reaching for him, but Sebastian caught my hand, drawing me back.

"Leave him be," he murmured into my hair as my

heart wrenched for the tiny maid who had saved us all. "We will see if he returns to us."

"Returns?" I couldn't tear my eyes from their twin still forms.

"Without a heart, a gargoyle won't live. His is broken. We will see if he can... mend." Sebastian's voice took on a deep timbre, and I realized I wasn't the only one grieving the loss of a dear friend. His was a poor explanation of the stone man's grief, but I understood what Sebastian was saying.

I blinked back another cascade of tears but had little control over them. As the drive cleared of bodies, my mind began to take stock. "Where is Amy?"

"The remaining wolves took her. Payment. For Granny Smythe."

"Oh. It's done."

He had said so before, when I'd asked but nothing from then had sunk in. Reality turned with the death of a loved one, reorganizing my perceptions of what was important. It felt as though this should be a big moment, but instead, I was numb.

As I had been when this all started.

Empty.

I stared at the house, no more than a charred skeleton against a muted sky. The back of the building appeared to have collapsed altogether. I swayed in Sebastian's arms, lacking the energy to ask anything more.

Charleton crouched before me, proffering a square of clean cloth that looked as though it might have been torn from the inside of his jacket. I took it gratefully, unable to give him even the faintest smile in thanks.

"Was this all worth it?" I whispered hoarsely.

Charleton looked at my maid and Dolion for a long moment. Then he knelt, his arms sliding beneath Minette's empty form. When I thought he might lift her body and take her to be buried somewhere, he shifted her closer to Dolion, tucking her against him in a cold, lifeless embrace. Then he stood. Shoulders bowed, he took a silent moment of respect and retreated toward the broken house.

Somehow, Charleton's silence meant more than anything else that had happened.

Sebastian traced beneath my lashes, his lips following his fingers with gentle kisses. "We don't always have choices, Gella. But the ones we get, we make the most of."

He swept his arms beneath me, carrying me across the drive to the garden, and placed me on the lawn. Wrapping his jacket around my shoulders, he left me to watch over our friends as he headed inside the remnants of the house where the stone foundations hadn't burned, returning with Charleton and a few other townsmen I didn't recognize. They spoke quietly and began to clean up the broken bodies of a witch and the people who detested her in death almost as much as they had in life.

I knew then that what we had forged together through magic and love would last forever. I would have given up the sun for the monster who loved me back, but he wasn't that sort of man he had become. I was far from the displaced orphan who had mounted the docks in New Orleans so many weeks ago, thrust into an uncertain life where worries of love were the farthest thing from my mind. In Sebastian I had discovered acceptance, endurance and adoration.

In him, I found family.

EPILOGUE

GISELLA

The townsfolk weren't the enemy I feared when our world brought demons to their doors.

In the wake of our calamity, Sebastian folded around me, expecting their harm to fall on both our shoulders, which we deserved.

Their blows never came.

Minette's body was shifted with the rest of the burning night's casualties to the lawn until we worked out logistics of gravesites. A place behind the maze that caught the morning light was chosen by the staff who could see and speak to their friends throughout the day. Who were we to object?

As much as I couldn't bear the sight of her sheet covered body, worse was Charleton and Sebastian's procession through the maze bearing Dolion in their straining arms, but they refused all assistance offered.

Pallbearers of a different sort, I was certain Sebastian could have borne the gargoyle alone, but Charleton refused to budge and so they shared the weight of the job.

Once they reached the fountain, they set the stone man on his pedestal where he overlooked the ash and smoke remains of the house. Unlike the staff, we buried Minette next to Dolion, and I planted irises and poppies around her, visiting them both each day as I wrote out the history I'd acquired of all who had fallen around Amy—Anitta–though I omitted her names from the pages, unwilling to mar their passing with the taint of what she made of the lives sacrificed in lieu of hers.

Instead of the fear and hatred we expected, the townsfolk adopted us, spent hours cleaning the house, the rooms that remained, helping us rebuild during daylight hours. More than one of the old and a few younger servants had told stories of Sebastian's strange sort of lordship and though the new world wasn't about the old ways, they seemed to see his new start as a chance at acceptance and welcomed us in.

While Sebastian worked on alone once the sun rested in the evenings, doubling their efforts, I sat in the evenings, filling in journal after journal. I barely saw him in those days. Charleton often accompanied him, working shoulder to shoulder in silence with his master, earning more than a friend's place at his side.

Knowledge of the night's event swarmed over the fledgling community. We were amazed at the assistance of the townspeople who helped rebuild the house once the greater structure was complete. What could have been ruined by fear created a foundation every person who worked on restoring the house made a claim on, and was welcomed in.

A turnabout on their respect, opening our arms to bring them in. Perhaps if that barrier of fear hadn't been there in the first place, the superstitions of old following us across oceans and a few extra monsters, we wouldn't have been in this position in the first place.

And so, with open secrets arming us all, Sebastian opened the doors once the building was complete, welcoming every person who placed a stone atop the walls into his existence, refusing to keep secrets. Inside I knew he was as torn and conflicted by the events. In hiding away from the world, he had created his own enemy. I was pleased to see him try something new in the aftermath.

Trust.

A new experience for him, but we made it work.

We sent word to the wolves, but they never responded, preferring to hide within the bayou's limits, protecting their own.

I didn't blame them in the least.

Removing the bodies that littered the drive was the first job we dealt with after the fire. I undertook the responsibility of ensuring their names and what stories of them we knew were recorded in the family bible, my task once the journals of that night's events were complete, and stored in the house's new library.

That I had once been exhausted by writing out invitations seemed a poor farce on my penance.

Each day, I sat with Minette and Dolion, waiting for the day the gargoyle's heart would heal, painting the gardens and the house to bring new memories to our home along with those not present to share it. My days and nights began to blur to match Sebastian's routine, and I would rest those few brief hours around daybreak until I could be with him again.

In time, a small girl with a head of dark hair to match Sebastian's came from a land far across the ocean to seek him as her final relative. Beside me she learned to talk to the stone man where he sat upon his fountain, telling him stories of fantasy lands and the town boys who teased her strange appearance and odd speech and unageing skin long after my accent faded along with my youth.

Dolion's presence remained a comfort to us both as she developed much slower and I grew older, and aged. All the while Sebastian, of course, remained the same.

Perhaps in some unknown future world, he would find peace as I had with my own immortal. Despite watching his face every day as the seasons passed, he never moved or changed, maintaining his penance over Minette's grave.

I hoped one day, his stone heart would learn to beat again.

I hope you enjoyed Gisella and Sebastian's story. Please leave a review. This story isn't over just yet.

Dolion will rise again with a beating heat
to complete the SILENT SENTINELS duet.
Read ECHOES OF THE VOID
Silent Sentinels Duet book 2

ABOUT THE AUTHOR

Raven Hush writes spicy paranormal romance and exists on a diet of red wine and coffee. When she isn't romancing the monster under her bed, she writes contemporary romance and suspense as *USA Today bestselling* author Sofia Aves and kidlit under a not-so-super-secret pen name. Raven lives at Romance Cafe Publishing in their Marketing and PR department.

Raven writes in her own dragon bookish cave and wrangles her alpacas daily. One day, she might even write about them.

www.sofiaaves.com